'Mr Brandon
a certain...s
received your

'It is most unusual for a schoolmistress to spend time alone with the parent of one of her girls,' she observed.

'I seldom trouble myself with what is or is not unusual, Miss de Coverdale,' Oliver replied blandly. 'I wished to speak to you alone and perceived this to be the best way of doing that.'

'But what did you wish to speak to me about?'

Oliver sent her a mocking glance. 'Do you really need to ask, given the nature of our first acquaintance?'

A young woman disappears.
A husband is suspected of murder.
Stirring times for all the neighbourhood in

Book 11

When the debauched Marquis of Sywell won
Steepwood Abbey years ago at cards, it led to the death
of the then Earl of Yardley. Now he's caused scandal
again by marrying a girl out of his class—and young
enough to be his granddaughter! After being married
only a short time, the Marchioness has disappeared,
leaving no trace of her whereabouts. There is every
expectation that yet more scandals will emerge, though
no one yet knows just how shocking they will be.

The four villages surrounding the Steepwood Abbey
estate are in turmoil, not only with the dire goings-on
at the Abbey, but also with their own affairs. Each
story in **The Steepwood Scandal** follows the mystery
behind the disappearance of the young woman, and the
individual romances of lovers connected in some way
with the intrigue.

Regency Drama
intrigue, mischief...and marriage

THE GUARDIAN'S DILEMMA

Gail Whitiker

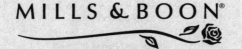

MILLS & BOON®

First published in Great Britain 2002
Harlequin Mills & Boon Limited,
Eton House, 18-24 Paradise Road, Richmond, Surrey TW9 1SR

© Harlequin Books S.A. 2002

Special thanks and acknowledgement are given to Gail Whitiker for her contribution to The Steepwood Scandal series.

ISBN 0 263 82852 2

Set in Times Roman 10½ on 12 pt.
119-0302-63107

Printed and bound in Spain
by Litografía Rosés S.A., Barcelona

Originally hailing from Pembrokeshire, **Gail Whitiker** now lives on beautiful Vancouver Island on the west coast of Canada. When she isn't indulging her love of writing, you'll find her enjoying brisk walks along the Island's many fine beaches, or trying to catch up on her second love: reading. She wrote her first novel when she was in her teens, and still blesses her English teacher for not telling her how bad it really was.

The Guardian's Dilemma features characters you will have already met in *A Most Improper Proposal*, Gail Whitiker's previous novel in **The Steepwood Scandal**.

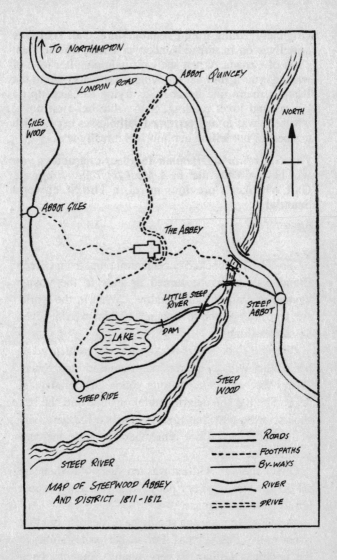

TO NORTHAMPTON

ABBOT QUINCEY

LONDON ROAD

NORTH

GILES
WOOD

ABBOT GILES

THE ABBEY

LITTLE STEEP
RIVER

STEEP
ABBOT

LAKE

DAM

STEEP
WOOD

STEEP RIDE

STEEP RIVER

MAP OF STEEPWOOD ABBEY
AND DISTRICT 1811 - 1812

ROADS
FOOTPATHS
BY-WAYS
RIVER
DRIVE

Chapter One

August 1812

'*Elope!*' The shocked exclamation burst from Oliver
Brandon's lips as he turned to stare at the young
woman standing by the window. 'What in the world
are you talking about, Sophie? Gillian would never
do such a thing.'

'Wouldn't she?' Mrs Sophie Llewellyn glanced at
her brother with an expression of amused indulgence.
'You know what a headstrong young girl our stepsister is. She has the determination of three and she has
shown in the past that if she is pushed too hard, she
will rebel. Do you not remember that little incident
several years ago?'

Oliver snorted. 'Gillian was ten years old when she
set off for Dover on her pony. At seventeen, I expect
her to have more sense.'

'And at seventeen she should have, dearest, but that
is not to say that she has. For all her protestations to
the contrary, Gillian is very young. She has been

pampered and cosseted most of her life and has not half the maturity you or I had at that age.'

Oliver's dark brows arched upwards in surprise. 'Are you saying I've spoiled her?'

'No, but she has certainly been indulged. And not only by you, so you needn't look at me like that.' Sophie's mouth twitched. 'I too am guilty of having given in to her whims. But Gillian has such a sweet, amiable nature that one cannot help oneself. However, you cannot deny that she likes to have her own way, Oliver, and when she doesn't get it, she can become...'

'Troublesome?'

'I prefer to use the word challenging.' Sophie smiled as if hoping to soften the criticism. 'Troublesome has such a disagreeable connotation to it, don't you think?'

'Hmm.' Oliver clasped his hands behind his back and joined his sister at the window. It was easy to discern the resemblance between the two. They both had the same dark, wavy hair and finely sculpted features of the Brandon side of the family, and the same height and physical stature of their late mother's Howden connections. But that was where the similarities ended. In matters of personality and temperament, they were as different as night and day. Oliver might be only four years older than his sister, but his brooding countenance and serious nature often made him appear considerably more.

At thirty-five, he was as fit as a man ten years his junior, but unlike such greenheads, there was nothing of the dandy about him. He did not wear his hair in a Brutus crop or pad his calves to show a shapelier leg. He had no need to, given his propensity for strenuous exercise, both in the boxing ring and with the foil. But he was not so easily moved to laughter as was his sister, nor so trusting of the outside world.

In contrast to both of them was their seventeen-year-old stepsister, Gillian Gresham; a blonde, blue-eyed child who no more resembled either of them than did a rose a cornstalk. She had the round face and bubbly personality of her late mother, and standing at just over five feet tall, she barely reached Oliver's shoulder. She was a happy, good-natured child, inclined, as Sophie had said, to cajole people into giving her what she wanted, but in such a way that no one could truly resent her for it. And she was forever falling in and out of love. Oliver had had more than his share of emotional battles with her over the past two years.

Gillian had come to live at Shefferton Hall when her mother, Catherine, had married Oliver's father just over nine years ago. She had become his legal ward when Catherine had succumbed to pneumonia two years later. Surprisingly, Oliver had grieved deeply over his stepmother's death. More so, perhaps, than he had over his own mother's. The bond between them had been surprisingly strong, and Oliver knew that Catherine had come to feel the same respect and admiration for him as he had for her. It was the reason she had left Gillian in his care, and that she had died at peace, secure in the knowledge that her only daughter would be well taken care of.

The guardianship hadn't been bad to begin with, Oliver admitted. Gillian had been an amusing little minx and, for the first few years, had behaved in a manner suitable to her age and in way that gave him little cause for concern. But over the last four years she had developed into a very determined young woman indeed. So much so that when she thought she was right, there was little hope of convincing her otherwise. At times, even his mild-mannered sister had been tempted to throw up her hands in despair.

At the moment, however, Gillian was happily engaged in the garden below, gathering a colourful selection of roses and placing them in a large straw basket. The fact that the basket was being held by a handsome officer who seemed only too happy to perform such a menial task accounted for a large part of *her* happiness, Oliver reflected moodily, and for considerably less of his.

'Challenging may be the more agreeable word, Sophie, but I think troublesome is the more appropriate one,' he muttered. 'At least when she was ten I had no need to worry about *who* she might be running off to Dover with.' Oliver's brow furrowed as he studied the disturbing scene below. 'I do not like Sidney Charles Wymington. I have no doubt he has a flattering tongue and that his looks are as elegant as anyone might wish, but his glib manner disturbs me very much. He is forever offering opinions on matters that do not concern him, and he is seldom caught without an answer. And I, for one, do not trust a man who is never at a loss for words.'

A twinkle appeared in the depths of Sophie's bright green eyes. 'You are seldom at a loss for words yourself, Oliver, and I have never held that against you.'

'Thank you, my dear, but I do not use my eloquence to curry favour as does Mr Wymington.' Oliver's mouth curved in a rueful smile. 'Nor, I think, do I do it half as well. He seems to live very comfortably for a half-pay officer, don't you think?'

Sophie lifted her elegantly clad shoulders in a shrug. 'I have heard that he does, though I have never stopped to consider the reasons why. However, if it makes you feel any better, Gillian has informed me that he is hopeful of a posting in the near future.'

'Really.' Oliver's dark eyes narrowed as he turned to look out the window again. 'If that is the case, it cannot come soon enough.'

It was not the first time Oliver had expressed negativity towards one of Gillian's suitors, nor the first time he had scoffed at her claims of the gentleman's being the most romantic in all England. Because Oliver himself was not a romantic. He and Sophie had been raised in a home where love and affection had had no place. His parents had tolerated one another, but there had been little more to their marriage than that. Perhaps that was why his father had not grieved overly much when his first wife had died only four years after Sophie had been born.

His father's second marriage, to Catherine Gresham, had started out better than his first, but it had not ended well. Catherine had died most unexpectedly of complications arising from an illness, and after that, Oliver's father had withdrawn even further into himself. So much so, that when he lost his life in a boating accident, many people wondered whether or not it had been a deliberate act of suicide.

Thank goodness his sister's marriage had turned out as well as it had, Oliver reflected now. Rhys Llewellyn had fallen in love with Sophie the first time he'd met her, and hadn't been in the least intimidated by her unusual height. Indeed, he had professed himself delighted to meet a lady who could look at him without risk of serious injury to her neck. More im-

portantly, he had called her beautiful at a time when
Sophie had been least willing to believe it, and in the
end, his repeated assurances had won her heart and
her hand.

Oliver had never experienced that kind of gentle,
all-encompassing love. Nor had he known the kind of
soul-searing passion that could turn one's heart and
one's life inside out. He knew what it was to experience physical desire, but he had sated those urges
with Nicolette, a pretty little ballet dancer who'd become his mistress the year he turned four-and-twenty.
He still frequented her bed whenever he felt the need
to lose himself in the softness of a woman's arms,
but other than that, there had been precious little female intrusion into his life. Which was probably why
his view of marriage as a whole was somewhat
tainted.

Oliver harboured no delusions that people wed
solely for love. He knew that women looked to marriage for social advancement and security, while
men—especially those in restricted financial circumstances—hoped to avail themselves of money and a
convenient lifestyle.

Sidney Charles Wymington was just such a man.
Oliver was sure of it. Which explained why he had
been less than pleased when Gillian had started coming to him with praises spilling from her lips about
the man. Why should he celebrate the fact that his
ward was keeping company with a fellow who had
little to recommend him other than his handsome face
and his practised charm?

After all, Gillian was an heiress. Her mother had
left her an inheritance of some twenty-five thousand
pounds, with the instructions that the money be re-

leased to her on the occasion of her twenty-first birth-day *or* upon the day she married; the latter proviso having been made in order to prevent Oliver from having to use his own funds to provide the necessary dowry. Catherine had been convinced of Oliver's suit-ability as a guardian for Gillian, and equally confident that he would *never* allow her to enter into an unac-ceptable alliance. As a result, she had put no further restrictions on the inheritance than that.

Therein lay the problem. Oliver had no idea whether Gillian had told Mr Wymington about the conditions of her inheritance, but he *did* know she hadn't troubled herself to conceal the depth of her feelings for him. And if it came right down to it, Oliver knew that Wymington wouldn't hesitate to use those feelings to his own advantage.

'Then what would you suggest I do, Sophie?' Oliver said at length, a note of frustration creeping into his voice. 'Gillian is headstrong, as you say, but I cannot believe she would knowingly disgrace her-self—or us—by doing something imprudent.'

'You are her legal guardian, Oliver. You could for-bid her to see him.'

'What, and run the risk of alienating her even fur-ther?' Oliver shook his head. 'I would far rather cast Mr Wymington in the role of the villain than myself. Unfortunately, I have checked into his military rec-ords and found nothing to condemn him, other than a slight propensity towards gambling.'

'Unless it is a propensity which causes him to lose vast sums of money in a single night, I doubt it will be enough to sway Gillian's opinion of him. Especially if she believes herself in love with him—'

'In love!'

'Well, you cannot ignore the possibility, my dear.'
Sophie's expression softened. 'You see how she behaves with him. Most young ladies would have the
good sense to conceal their affections, but Gillian
seems to want *everyone* to know how she feels about
the man. Which is why I think it would be a good
idea if you were to separate them for a while.'

'And how do you suggest I do that? Even if I were
to tell Wymington to keep away from Gillian, I do
not trust him to listen to me.'

Sophie sighed her agreement. 'I doubt he would. If
Mr Wymington knows that Gillian is an heiress and
his intentions are what you say, he will be more than
willing to bide his time. He will have to if you do
not intend to give your approval to the match.'

'Unless he decides to elope with her, as you suggested earlier. Which given the terms of Catherine's
will *any* man might be tempted to do. '

Sophie had the grace to look embarrassed. 'Well,
perhaps I was being a touch melodramatic in saying
that she would elope. For all Gillie's headstrong
ways, I do not believe she would knowingly disgrace
us. But I still think it would be wise to send her away
for a while. With any luck, her absence will force Mr
Wymington to look elsewhere for a wealthy bride,
and give Gillian time to come to her senses.'

'That's all very well, my dear, but where do you
suggest I send her? She has no family who would
welcome her. At least, none whom I would trust not
to try to take advantage of her fortune themselves.'

'You could send her away to school,' Sophie said
slowly. 'Do you remember me telling you about the
Guarding Academy for Girls?'

Oliver began to pace. 'No. Should I?'

'I suppose not. A friend of mine, Lady Brookwell, mentioned it to me in passing a few weeks back. She said that her eldest daughter, Elizabeth, was there and that she was very pleased with her progress. The headmistress is a woman by the name of Eleanor Guarding and from what Lady Brookwell tells me, she is quite a unique person. Not at all the sort one usually finds running schools of this nature.'

Oliver stopped pacing. 'And where is this Guarding's Academy for Girls?'

'In Northamptonshire. I believe Steep Abbot is the name of the village.'

'Steep Abbot?' He frowned. 'Why would that name be familiar to me?'

'Possibly because it is where the Marquis of Sywell was murdered three months ago.'

'Good God! And you would have me send Gillian there?'

Sophie chuckled as she let the curtain fall back across the window. 'I hardly think Gillie is in danger of suffering a similar fate, my dear. From all I've heard, Sywell was not undeserving of his reward. But the reason I mention it is because the teachers at the Academy are purported to be more liberal-minded than most. They strive to impress upon their girls the importance of thinking for themselves.'

Oliver sent her a sharp glance. 'Gillian does quite enough thinking for herself as it is, Sophie. That is one of the problems I am trying to overcome.'

'You miss my point, dearest.' Sophie walked back towards the green velvet settee and sat down. 'The staff at Guarding's attempt to expand the intellectual minds of their pupils by providing tutelage in subjects not normally offered to young ladies. How many schools do you know of, for example, where girls are given extensive instruction in advanced mathematics and archaeology, as well as in Latin, Greek and philosophy? And from what I understand, Mrs Guarding is herself something of an emancipationist and historian.'

'A female emancipationist?' Oliver frowned. 'The last thing I need is someone else filling Gillian's head with nonsense. I suspect Mr Wymington does quite enough of that as it is.'

'All right. Then what would you say if I told you that the teachers at the Guarding Academy would be far more likely to impress upon Gillian the importance of knowing what she stands to gain *and* to lose in a marriage to a man who is not her social or financial equal, than would a teacher in a fancy London seminary?'

Oliver thought about that for a moment. Sophie was an intelligent woman and he respected her opinion, but sending Gillian away to a girls' school was not going to be easy. He knew that in his ward's mind she had long ago finished with that kind of schooling. 'What could I say that would persuade her to go?'

'That, I'm afraid, is something you are going to have to work out for yourself, Oliver. I merely put forward the suggestion as a solution to the problem of how to separate Gillian from Mr Wymington for a while.' Sophie smiled as she rose to kiss her brother affectionately on the cheek. 'After all, a year spent at a boarding school might be time enough for her to see the gentleman in a different light. And if Mr Wymington is the adventurer you think, it may be all the time we need.'

* * *

Oliver gave his sister's words considerable thought over the next few days, and the more he thought about it, the more he came to see that the plan had merit. Gillian had always resented the fact that young ladies were not offered the same quality of education as young gentlemen, and by the sound of things, spending the better part of a year at Mrs Guarding's Academy would give her precisely that opportunity.

In the end, however, it did not come down to a matter of choice as to whether or not he sent her away to school, but rather, how quickly could he get her there. Gillian's conversations were becoming far too full of Mr Wymington for Oliver's liking. It seemed that every utterance was prefaced by 'Mr Wymington said this,' or 'Mr Wymington thinks that,' until by the end of the week Oliver was sick to death of hearing about Mr Wymington. But even in his frustration, he saw the way Gillian's face closed down whenever he expressed negativity towards the man, and knew that he was fighting a losing battle.

It was that stubbornness which convinced him that Sophie was right. Gillian *was* impulsive, and she was used to getting her own way. She was also at the age where, like most young women, her thoughts were turning more frequently towards marriage. Oliver could not be sure that if he pushed her too hard, she wouldn't do precisely what Sophie had suggested and elope.

For that reason, little more than a week after his conversation with her, he contacted the headmistress at the Guarding Academy for Girls in Steep Abbot, and then, a few days later, told Gillian of his plans.

Needless to say, she was not pleased.

'You intend to send me *where*?' she echoed in disbelief.

'It is called Mrs Guarding's Academy for Girls,' Oliver informed her calmly. 'I thought that since you did not have occasion to finish your lessons with Monsieur Deauvall and Miss Berkmore, you might welcome the opportunity to do so now.'

'But I have no wish to go to school!' Gillian cried petulantly. 'I am nearly eighteen years of age, Oliver! I have far more important things on my mind than silly lessons. Mr Wymington says—'

'I don't give a…that is to say,' Oliver said, catching himself just in time, 'I don't think anything Mr Wymington has to say on the matter is relevant, Gillian. I am your legal guardian and I will be the one to decide how and where you complete your education. And after due consideration, I have determined that the Guarding Academy is the place for you to do that.'

Gillian stamped her dainty little foot and set her blonde curls dancing. 'But I don't want to go to any stuffy girls' school!'

'From all I've heard, the school is anything but stuffy. The headmistress is a female emancipationist and the teachers are all somewhat radical in their thinking. A young lady with your intelligence and personality should get on very well there.'

'But I do not wish—'

'Gillian, the discussion is at an end. We leave for Steep Abbot in a week's time. I have already sent a letter to Mrs Guarding advising her of your enrolment, and have received a letter back confirming your place. I would advise you to make whatever arrangements you feel are necessary and then tell me when you are ready to depart.'

Gillian's face darkened. 'What about Mr Wymington?'

'What about him?'

'Oh, how can you be so heartless, Oliver! You must know that I care for him. And it cannot have escaped your notice that he holds me in considerable esteem.'

'It hasn't escaped my notice at all, but neither has the fact that you are only seventeen.'

'I shall be eighteen in January, but what has that to do with it? Jane Twickingham was betrothed to Lord Hough when she was only sixteen, and you have told me yourself she was a silly little chit. What has my age to do with Mr Wymington's courting me?'

Oliver's eyes turned the colour of stone. 'Since when did Mr Wymington's visits take on the aspect of a courtship? He has not sought my permission to address you.'

As if realising she had said more than she should, Gillian's pretty cheeks flushed. 'Well, no, of course not, because we are only acquaintances. But that is not to say that I...that is, that he—'

'Gillian, what do you really know of Mr Wymington?' Oliver asked, deciding to try a different approach. 'That he is charming, I have no doubt. That he knows how to turn a young girl's head, I have seen with my own eyes. But what do you *know* of the man's character or background? Has he spoken to you of his family? Do you know where he comes from or who his people are?'

'Of course I do.' Gillian lifted her chin in defiance. 'We have spoken of all those things. Mr Wymington has nothing to hide from me.'

'Then what has he told you of himself?'

'That his parents are dead, and that he has a sister living in Cornwall to whom he is not close. He also told me he has hopes of achieving a higher rank in the militia.'

'I see. And what is he now—a lieutenant?'

'Yes.'

'Has he the funds to purchase his next commission?'

'I do not believe he has,' Gillian admitted reluctantly, 'but he did tell me he was like to come into a considerable amount of money.'

Oliver was immediately on his guard. 'Did he say how?'

'Well, no, not precisely.'

'Did he say *when* he might expect this good fortune?'

Gillian coloured. 'No, nor did I ask. Why should I when one day I shall have money enough for us both?'

That was precisely what Oliver had been afraid of hearing. 'And I suppose you told him that?'

'Yes.' Gillian's golden brows drew together in a frown. 'Why would I not?'

Oliver suppressed a sigh. There was no point in answering the question. His naïve young ward might not realise how tempting was the carrot she dangled in front of Mr Wymington's nose, but he certainly did. 'I'm sorry, Gillian, my mind is made up. We leave for Steep Abbot in a week's time. Say goodbye to whichever friends you wish to and then begin your preparations to leave.'

'But—'

'And you are not to see Mr Wymington again.'

'But that is not fair, Oliver! Why can I not say goodbye to him? He is a friend, and you told me I may say goodbye to whomever I wished.'

'You know very well I was not referring to gentlemen when I said that. You may write Mr Wymington a farewell note, but that is all. And I wish to read it before you send it away.'

Oliver could see that Gillian was angry. There was a defiant sparkle in her bright blue eyes and her chin was thrust out in the gesture he had come to know so well.

'I think you are being beastly about this, Oliver,' she flung at him. 'You are sending me away to some dreadful school because you do not like Mr Wymington and because you do not wish me to see him.'

'I am sending you to Steep Abbot so that you may complete your education,' Oliver replied with equanimity. 'I do not share in the opinion that all a young lady need know how to do is arrange flowers and engage in polite conversation. You are far too bright for that, as you yourself have told me on more than one occasion.'

'I do not have to listen to you!'

'Ah, but you do. At least until the occasion of your twenty-first birthday. I promised your mother that I would look after you until that time, and I intend to keep my word. Now, I would ask you to respect my wishes and abide by my instructions. We leave in six days.'

'Six!' Gillian's eyes widened in dismay. 'You said we were leaving in seven!'

'I was, but your decision to argue has persuaded me to move it up a day.'

'But you cannot—'

'And for every objection you make, we shall leave one day sooner. The choice is yours, Gillian.'

With that Oliver turned and walked towards the door. He could feel his ward's eyes boring into his back, but he did not give way. He had learned that the only way to deal with Gillian was to be firm, regardless of what Sophie or anyone else thought. He was doing what was best for the girl and with any luck, she would eventually come to realise that.

In the interim, it did not lessen his awareness that had looks been sufficient to kill, he would have been lying on the floor suffering his final moments even now!

Chapter Two

September 1812

Helen de Coverdale sat in the small, walled garden behind the main body of the school building and breathed a sigh of pure pleasure.

What a glorious morning it had turned out to be! With the sun so warm and the air so mild, it was hard to believe that the first of September had already come and gone. In fact, if she closed her eyes and tried very hard, she could almost convince herself that it was the fragrance of spring flowers perfuming the air rather than the dusky scent of autumn signalling the end of yet another summer.

How quickly time passed, Helen thought wistfully as she gazed out towards the gardens. Indeed, with the arrival of each new year, the days seemed to tumble over one another with ever-increasing speed. When she was a child, the summers had stretched on endlessly. She remembered long, golden afternoons spent in the Italian countryside, when there had been nothing more pressing to do than paint pictures of olive groves and fields of brightly coloured flowers. She remembered sitting with her grandmother in the little stone house, listening to her tell the same wonderful stories she had told Helen's own mother when she had been a child growing up there. How blissful those days seemed now, and how very long ago. Before the long years of war had begun to change everything.

Thank goodness her memories of the past hadn't changed, Helen reflected silently. They would always be there for her, reminding her of a time when her future had loomed bright and hopeful. Before the heartbreak of love and the harsh realities of life had intruded to shatter her expectations and chase away her dreams.

Helen picked up the letter she had placed on the seat beside her and smiled as she read it over one more time. It was from her dear friend Desirée Nash. Desirée lived in London now, but before that she too had been a teacher at the Guarding Academy. She had taught Latin, Greek and philosophy for over six years, until a most unfortunate incident had forced her to leave.

Helen's smile faded as she thought back to that dreadful time. In the spring of last year, Desirée had been caught in a compromising position with the father of one of the students. The fact that she had been completely innocent of any wrongdoing meant nothing. The episode had been witnessed by Mrs Guarding and two of the girls, and it had effectively put an end to Desirée's future at the school. It had also been a particularly difficult time for Helen. She and Desirée had become close in the brief time they'd known each other, and Helen had shed many a tear

as a result of her friend being so cruelly sent away.
But she knew there was nothing she could have done.
There was nothing anyone could have done. It was
simply the way young single women were misused
by society.

But now, Desirée was having the last laugh on
them all. She had gone up to London and become the
companion of an aristocratic lady, and had then fallen
in love with the lady's dashing young nephew. Now,
she was betrothed to marry him. Her letter was to
inform Helen of the date of the wedding, and to say
how very much she hoped her dear friend would be
able to come up to London for it.

Helen sighed as she carefully refolded the letter.
How wonderful it would be to go to London and see
Desirée married. How satisfying to see her take her
place in society as Lady Buckworth. Indeed, after everything she had endured, it seemed only right and
fitting that she should. Unfortunately, as much as
Helen would have loved to go, she knew it was impossible. The school was operating short of the full
complement of teachers as it was, and there were new
girls arriving all the time. Mrs Guarding had informed
them that three new girls would be coming in at the
end of this week alone.

Which simply meant there was no way Helen could
take the time necessary to attend Desirée's wedding.
She could not afford to risk losing her position here.
While she knew that being a teacher was not a pro-
fession many people would envy, it was all she had,
and in her own way she was happy with it. She valued
the company and friendship of the other women who
worked here; women who, like herself, had been
forced to make their own way in the world. And it

was certainly a vast improvement from the positions she had held in the past. Better to be a schoolmistress in a country school than a governess in a fine house where one lived in constant fear of being caught alone by the master.

'Helen, Helen, come quickly. Mrs Guarding is looking for you!'

Helen looked up to see Jane Emerson hurrying across the grass towards her. Jane was a pretty little thing with big brown eyes and dark hair. She taught dance and deportment at Mrs Guarding's and was well liked by both the staff and the girls. But her appearance in the garden now with the news that Mrs Guarding wanted to see her came as something of a surprise.

'But why would she wish to see me?' Helen asked, hastily slipping the letter into her pocket. 'I have no classes until this afternoon.'

'Yes, but Miss Gresham and her father are here.'

Helen blinked. 'Miss Gresham?'

'One of the new girls.' Jane stopped for a moment to catch her breath. 'Mrs Guarding is gathering...everyone in the hall to meet them.'

'But I thought none of the new girls were due to arrive until the end of the week?'

'That was what Mrs Guarding told us, but Miss Gresham is here now and we must all take our places. Come, Helen, we had best make haste,' Jane urged. 'You know how Mrs Guarding hates to be kept waiting!'

'I apologise for our early arrival, Mrs Guarding,' Oliver told the headmistress in the privacy of her sitting-room, 'but I thought it best that Gillian begin her studies here as soon as possible.'

Mrs Guarding inclined her head. 'No apology is necessary, Mr Brandon. I have asked my staff to assemble downstairs and it will be only a few moments before they are there. But in the interim, is there anything you would like to tell me about your ward?'

Oliver glanced at the older woman in surprise. 'Why would you ask?'

'Because given Gillian's age, I thought there might have been another reason for your haste in bringing her here.'

'I'm not sure I take your meaning.'

The headmistress looked at him in the same manner she might have regarded a tardy pupil. 'Mr Brandon, I am very proud of the reputation I have built here at Guarding's, but I am well aware that education is not the only reason parents send their daughters away. Especially to a school like this.'

'Like this?'

'Yes. One where the main focus is *not* to prepare young women for marriage.'

As a man accustomed to plain speaking, Oliver appreciated the headmistress's forthright style. He was also glad he had left Gillian in the corridor beyond. 'You are quite right, Mrs Guarding. I did have another reason for bringing my stepsister here, and under the circumstances, I see no reason why you should not be made aware of it.' He paused, took a deep breath, and then laced his hands together behind his back. 'Gillian has developed an unfortunate *tendre* for a gentleman of whom I do not approve. I had hoped that by separating them for a while, she might eventually find her affections cooling, and that the gentleman might find another target for his.'

A gleam of understanding appeared in the headmistress's eyes. 'Am I to assume that your ward's inheritance has something to do with the gentleman's interest?'

'I believe it has. Because of her wealth, Gillian will be pursued by a great many gentlemen. Some will love her for who she is while others will court her for what she has. I am hoping that when the time comes for her to make a choice, she will have the maturity and good sense to recognise the difference. At the moment, she hasn't,' Oliver said flatly. 'She has been swept away by the romantic ramblings of a handsome officer and believes herself in love with him. That is why I have brought her here.'

'I see.'

'It is also why I would like to make a request of you.'

'And that is?'

'The gentleman's name is Sidney Charles Wymington. He's a dashing fellow to be sure, but I want it made clear that Gillian is to have absolutely nothing to do with him.'

Mrs Guarding's eyebrows rose in inquiry. 'Have you reason to believe he would attempt to contact her here?'

'Regrettably, I have no reason not to believe it,' Oliver replied without hesitation. 'Mr Wymington has become rather persistent of late in his attentions. That is why Gillian is not to be allowed contact with any gentlemen who might call for her. She is also not to receive correspondence from anyone other than family members and female friends.'

Mrs Guarding nodded. 'I will ensure that my staff are made aware of your wishes, Mr Brandon.'

Oliver hesitated, not sure whether he detected a note of censure in the woman's voice, and even less sure why he should be disturbed by it. 'It is not my intention to sound like an overbearing parent, Mrs Guarding. Gillian is an amiable child but at times she can be…impulsive.' He gave the headmistress a rueful smile. 'She has done an excellent job of winding her tutors and her family around her little finger, and I regret to say she has become accustomed to getting her own way. I simply wish to prevent her from making a terrible mistake.'

The reluctant explanation brought a smile to Mrs Guarding's face. 'I understand your dilemma, Mr Brandon. It is an unfortunate truth that all too often young women are guided by their feelings rather than by their good sense, and I would not wish to see your ward come to grief. However, having said that, I must remind you that Miss Gresham is not a prisoner here. I cannot restrict all of her activities nor force her to remain on school property. If she is not to leave the grounds or to venture into the village unescorted, you must be the one to tell her that. I shall then endeavour to enforce your instructions as best I can.'

'That is only fair,' Oliver conceded. 'Gillian is well aware of my feelings regarding Mr Wymington, but as I've said, she's a strong-willed girl used to getting her own way. I am hoping that you and your staff will be able to strengthen and refine certain aspects of her character. I have been assured that moral development and intellectual growth are encouraged here.' Oliver took a deep breath. 'I wish her to understand that a young lady in possession of a considerable fortune cannot always be ruled by her heart, since the gentlemen who are courting her seldom are.'

Helen accompanied Jane to the dining-hall and smiled at the other teachers who were gathered there. They were a quiet group of women, made that way by their upbringing as much as by their choice of livelihood. They had all been forced to seek employment as a result of neither having had the good fortune to secure a husband, nor being in the enviable position of not needing one.

Helen had come to the Guarding Academy with a slight advantage over the others in that she had once been a pupil here. But she had never had cause to regret her decision. Even now, as she approached the beginning of her third year, she still enjoyed the opportunity of working with the young women in her care. That was not to say that all the young ladies *liked* being shown the best way to apply watercolours to a page, or how to conjugate Italian verbs. Indeed, with travel on the Continent so restricted, many of them felt there was little need for any language other than French in their daily lives, and some even balked at the learning of that.

For all of the attendant aggravations, however, Helen was not unhappy. There was a sense of belonging here; a feeling that they were all part of a small community, and that was important to Helen. She had spent too many lonely years forced to live without it.

The sound of approaching footsteps caused the low murmur of voices to cease, and in silent expectation the ladies turned towards the door where three people had just entered. Mrs Guarding led the way, followed by a very pretty young woman of about sixteen, and behind her, a gentleman who looked to be somewhere in his late thirties.

The young lady was dressed in the first style of fashion, from the brim of her attractive straw bonnet to the tips of her dark brown kid boots. She wore a short pelisse of deep lilac trimmed with white, and her light blonde hair was attractively arranged in loose curls around her face. She had high, round cheeks, a pert little nose, and a soft, rosebud mouth. But Helen could tell from the petulant expression on that mouth that the young lady was anything but pleased at the prospect of becoming a pupil at Mrs Guarding's Academy.

The gentleman behind her was equally well dressed. He was garbed in a dark blue jacket over fawn-coloured breeches, and was wearing a pair of highly polished Hessians. The perfectly tailored garments accentuated the width of his shoulders and the musculature of his legs, but there was nothing foppish about him. The fabric of his single-breasted waistcoat was tastefully subdued, while his snowy white cravat was well but not fussily tied.

Unfortunately, it was not the manner of his dress that gave Helen cause for alarm. As she slowly raised her eyes to his face, icy fingers tightened around her heart, and for a moment, she could scarcely breathe.

No! It could not be! Not now, after all this time, surely it was not him…

'Ladies, thank you for gathering so promptly,' Mrs Guarding began in her usual brisk manner. 'I am very pleased to introduce our newest student, Miss Gillian Gresham. Miss Gresham comes to us from Hertfordshire and will remain with us until the spring.

I know you will all make her feel welcome at the Guarding Academy.'

The young lady introduced as Miss Gresham glanced briefly at the cluster of women in the room, but she did not smile, nor did she respond to a whispered comment made by the gentleman beside her. She kept her eyes on the floor, refusing to look up or even to acknowledge him.

Helen bit her lip. She wished with all her heart that she *could* smile, but her face was frozen from top to bottom. *Dear heavens, was the gentleman truly the young woman's father? She would not have thought him old enough…*

'I would also like to introduce Mr Oliver Brandon, Miss Gresham's guardian,' Mrs Guarding went on to say. 'Mr Brandon has been good enough to donate an excellent selection of books from his own library for our use, and we are exceedingly grateful to him for his kindness. And now, Miss Gresham, Mr Brandon, if you would be so good as to follow me, I shall introduce you to the members of my staff.'

Helen nervously clasped her hands in front of her as the three began their perambulation. She kept her eyes down, wishing with all her heart that she could turn and run from the room, but she knew she dare not. Mrs Guarding would never forgive such a breach of etiquette from a member of her staff. Worse, it would only serve to draw attention to herself, and that was the last thing Helen wished to do. Which meant that she would just have to stay and see it through.

Perhaps he would not recognise her, she thought with sudden hope. After all, it had been nearly twelve years since he had last seen her and her appearance had certainly changed from the time she was a young woman of nineteen. There was also the possibility that he might not remember her, given that the room in which he'd found her had been very dark. And considering the awkwardness of the situation, he could have had only the briefest glimpse of her before—

'And this is Miss Helen de Coverdale,' she heard Mrs Guarding say. 'Miss de Coverdale has been with us for two years and instructs the girls in the areas of watercolours and Italian.'

Helen was aware of Miss Gresham and her guardian stopping in front of her and knew there was nothing she could do but acknowledge the introduction. She slowly raised her head and smiled tentatively at the young woman. 'Good morning, Miss Gresham.'

'Good morning,' came the lack-lustre reply.

Finally, with a reluctance borne of fear, Helen turned her head and looked at Oliver Brandon, trying all the while to ignore the butterflies swirling madly inside her stomach.

He, too, had changed over the past twelve years. His face, a striking mixture of lines and angles, was no longer that of a youth but of a man; one who had experienced life, both the good and the bad of it. He had a slender nose poised above a firm chin, a beautifully sculpted mouth and eyes that glowed a rich shade of brown. His hair was so dark as to appear almost black, as were his brows and lashes.

And he was tall. Helen had to tilt her head back to look into his face. Unfortunately, as she did, she saw the change in his expression, and felt her breath catch painfully in her throat. She recognised a brief flicker of surprise, followed by confusion, and then disbelief as forgotten memories stirred to life like the cold ashes of a long dead fire.

Helen's heart plummeted. It seemed that her hopes of escaping recognition were to be dashed. The man knew exactly who she was. And it was clear from the look on his face that time notwithstanding, he thought no better of her now than he had all those years ago.

Oliver stared at the young woman standing before him and felt as though he'd gone tumbling backwards in time.

Good God, was it really her? After all these years, could it possibly be the same woman?

He blinked hard, wondering if it was just his memory playing tricks on him. It had, after all, been years since he'd last seen her, and what he had seen of her at the time hadn't been all that much. But if it wasn't the same woman, it could surely have been her twin. The resemblance was uncanny. She had the same dark, lustrous hair and the same exotic beauty of the woman he had encountered so briefly all those years ago. But if it was the same woman, what the hell was she doing here?

How had a nobleman's whore become a teacher at a private girls' school?

'Mrs Guarding, might I have a word with you in your study?' Oliver said finally.

The headmistress glanced briefly at Miss de Coverdale, and then nodded. 'By all means, Mr Brandon. Miss Emerson, would you be so kind as to show Miss Gresham to her room?'

'Yes, Mrs Guarding.'

'Thank you, ladies. You may all return to your classes.'

As silent as little grey mice, the teachers filed out. Oliver saw a few cast surreptitious glances his way, but he noticed that none of them met his eye. And Helen de Coverdale did not look at him at all. She turned and walked away, not scurrying as the others had, but seeming to float across the floor, her movements slow and graceful, indicative of a poise and refinement he would not have expected in one of her class. At the door, she hesitated.

Oliver held his breath. Would she turn and look at him? If she did, it would be tantamount to an admission of familiarity. He waited as the seconds seemed to drag into hours.

In the end, she did not turn. Helen de Coverdale left the room and quietly closed the door behind her. She did not look back at him once.

Oliver slowly let go the breath he'd been holding. *It had to be her.* He'd seen the tell-tale flash of recognition in her eyes. She'd known who he was as surely as he'd known who *she* was. Which meant that his suspicions had to be right.

Helen de Coverdale *was* the young woman he'd stumbled upon in a darkened library, clutched in the passionate embrace of the married lord who had employed her.

Helen sat on the stone bench in the rose garden and thought back to the one and only time she had seen Oliver Brandon. It seemed a lifetime ago now, and in many ways, it was. She had been employed as a governess to Lord and Lady Talbot at the time. A dreadful position, and one which, had she had a choice, she would have turned and run away from as far and as fast as her legs would have carried her. Unfortunately, she hadn't had a choice. She had taken the job because she'd needed money to live on after her father had died. But she had seen the look in Lord Talbot's eyes the first time he had spoken to her, and had known what it would portend. Men had been looking at her like that since she was a child of thirteen, their hungry eyes lingering on her face and on her already ripening body.

Helen hadn't always had to worry about her appearance, of course. Before her father had died, her life had been very different. Robert de Coverdale had been a barrister, and as his only daughter, Helen had been a most eligible young lady. Indeed, her father had held out great hopes of her achieving a respectable marriage, perhaps even to a titled gentleman of some fortune.

What he had *not* expected was to see his only daughter fall in love with an impoverished clergyman who had come to the village during the summer of her seventeenth year.

Helen shuddered as she cast her mind back to her youth. Her father had refused to countenance an alliance between his daughter and Thomas Grant, the young vicar who'd claimed to love her. He'd said it was so far beneath her as to be laughable, and he had forbidden Helen to see him. And dutiful daughter that she was, Helen had obeyed. But it had taken years to recover from the heartache of losing Thomas. He had been her first true love, and the loss of that love had nearly destroyed her.

Over the next two years, more unhappiness had plagued Helen's life. Her mother had died in a freak riding accident, and her father, devastated by the loss of the woman he had loved more than life itself, had fallen into a series of personal and financial disasters. Unable to cope with a life in ruin, he had eventually taken his own life, and suddenly, Helen had discovered what it was to be dependent upon others. She'd had no relations in England. Her mother's family was still in Italy, and her father's only brother had been killed in the Americas. She'd had no one to turn to and no reputable avenues left open to her. It was then she started trying to disguise her natural beauty. She'd had no wish to appear attractive to the men who passed her in the street, or desirable to the husbands of other women.

Unfortunately, not even the wearing of plain clothes or the scraping back of her hair into a matronly style had been enough to disguise the true loveliness of her features. Helen had not been able to make her heavily lashed eyes appear any the less noticeable, or her full-lipped mouth any the less appealing. She hadn't been able to hide the fact that she wasn't as slim and dainty as were so many of the English ladies she met. She had inherited her mother's lush, exotic beauty, and it was that lushness which men found so attractive, Lord Talbot included. He had been hosting a shooting party at his country estate in Somerset that fateful weekend. The huge house had been filled with guests, many of whom had come all the way from Scotland to partake of the sport and to enjoy the lavish entertainments Lady Talbot had planned for the evenings.

Helen had not been invited to enjoy any of the amusements, of course. She had been included in the outing to Grovesend Hall simply to look after the children, but as a lowly governess she was not expected to participate in any of the festivities. So after tucking her two little girls into bed, she had gone down to the kitchen for a glass of warm milk and had then headed for the library. Lady Talbot had told Helen she could avail herself of his lordship's libraries. She had discovered Helen's passion for reading, and had assured her that as long as the master was not about, she was welcome to browse through his extensive selection of books.

Helen often wondered if Lady Talbot had known of her husband's philandering ways and had simply turned a blind eye to it. Whatever the case, Helen had made a terrible mistake that night. Believing that Lord Talbot would be busy entertaining his guests, she had made her way to the library—which was located well away from the source of the revelry—and had begun to look for something to read.

That was where Lord Talbot had found her.

Helen shivered as she went over it again in her mind. She remembered turning around at the sound of the door opening and seeing the look on his face; a look that had caused her to immediately forget all about books. Like most of the gentlemen, Lord Talbot had been drinking since noon and was well on his way to being in his cups. Knowing that, she had pulled her shawl more closely around her, had quickly retrieved her candle and her drink, and had gone to move past him.

For a drunkard, Lord Talbot had moved with terrifying speed. The milk and the candle had gone flying as Talbot pulled her roughly into his arms and started kissing her.

Repulsed, Helen had struggled against him, fighting to avoid the wet, slobbering kisses he had pressed upon her neck and mouth. She'd sensed that her struggles were only adding to his excitement, however, and given that he had the advantage of both size and weight, Helen had been left in no doubt as to the outcome. He pushed her back towards the settee, his mouth smothering the scream that left her throat as his other hand closed painfully over her breast.

At that precise moment, the door to the library had opened and Oliver Brandon had walked in.

Helen hadn't known who he was at the time. He had simply been a guest in her employer's home. But during the long, agonising moments in which he'd stood frozen in the doorway, Helen had seen the look of shock on his face. And she had watched it change to one of disgust as he'd placed his own interpretation upon the scene before him. He'd muttered an apology and abruptly withdrawn, not even guessing at the true nature of the horror taking place.

Helen closed her eyes as the humiliating memories came flooding back. The only good thing about it was that Mr Brandon's appearance—however brief—had given her the chance she'd needed to escape. Distracted by the sound of the intrusion, Lord Talbot had momentarily looked up, and in doing so, had loosened his grip. In that blessed moment, Helen had broken free and bolted for the door. She had raced towards the stairs as tears of anger and humiliation had streamed down her face and had run all the way to her room. Once inside, she'd turned the key in the lock, wedged a small writing-table against the door and pushed the bed against that. She hadn't slept a wink all night.

The next morning, she'd left Grovesend Hall for ever. She had returned to London, where she had lived off her wits until she had been able to secure another position in the south of England. She had never seen Lord or Lady Talbot again. She hadn't seen Oliver Brandon either. Until this morning, when he had brought his sixteen-year-old ward to be a student at Mrs Guarding's Academy.

But it had been clear from the look on his face that he had not forgotten who *she* was. And he would surely be wondering how and why a woman of such loose morals had ended up becoming a teacher in a private girls' school. Especially one where he was intending to leave his own stepsister as a pupil.

Chapter Three

Oliver was silent as he accompanied the headmistress back to her study. His mind was spinning, turning over in ever-increasing detail the memories of that fateful night so very long ago.

He had never forgotten what he had seen in the library at Grovesend Hall. He remembered with distaste the sight of Lord Talbot's hand clutching the young woman's breast, and the lustful expression on his face when he'd turned around and seen Oliver standing there. Even now, the memory of it repulsed him.

The problem was, Oliver hadn't known William Talbot well at the time. Yes, they had frequented the same clubs, and they'd often run into one another at social occasions, but the difference in their ages had prevented them from forming any kind of a close friendship. But for whatever reason, Talbot had taken a liking to him and Oliver had been young enough to be flattered by his regard. So when the wealthy peer had invited him to come to his country house for a weekend shooting party, Oliver had accepted with alacrity.

He shook his head now, as he so often did when he thought back to the naïveté of his youth. He hadn't known that Talbot was such a reprobate. But even if he had, Oliver would never have expected the man to flaunt his mistress in front of his guests during a crowded soirée. What would his wife have said if *she'd* been the one to discover them in the library?

Fortunately, or unfortunately, it hadn't been Lord Talbot's wife who had stumbled upon that sorry sight, but Oliver himself. He had opened the door to the library, wanting only to escape from the noise and revelry going on in the other rooms, and had come face to face with his host and a young woman locked in a passionate embrace. Obviously, the sound of his arrival had immediately served to catch the young woman's attention, if not Talbot's, and she had glanced up and stared at him across the darkened room.

For the space of moments, Oliver had been treated to the sight of one of the loveliest faces he had ever seen. A cascade of thick, black hair fell nearly to her waist, framing a face of such arresting beauty that he felt as though he was staring into the face of an angel. Her dark eyes had reached into his soul, tugging at the very core of who he was.

The memory of those eyes had stayed with him for years.

Then, belatedly aware that he had stumbled upon a lover's tryst, Oliver had withdrawn. He'd closed the door and gone back to the ballroom, trying to lose himself in the crowd of revellers and merrymakers. But for some reason, the memory of what he'd seen had stayed with him, disturbing him to such a degree that even he himself hadn't been able to explain it.

The next morning, he'd left Grovesend Hall and headed back to London. He hadn't said a word to anyone about what he'd seen. Not even to Lord Talbot who, obviously too drunk to remember, had been surprised and disappointed by his young guest's hasty departure. Nor had he seen the raven-haired beauty again.

Until this morning when he had arrived at Mrs Guarding's Academy for Girls. Her name was Helen de Coverdale. And unless he did something about it, she was about to become one of the women who would have a direct influence on his impressionable young ward.

'You wished to speak with me, Mr Brandon?'

'Hmm?' Oliver glanced across at the headmistress, and realised she had been waiting for him to begin. 'Oh. Yes. I wanted to ask you about…one of your teachers.'

'Miss de Coverdale.'

It wasn't a question and Oliver frowned. 'How did you know?'

'Because she was the only one who elicited any kind of response from you. Forgive me for speaking plainly, Mr Brandon, but are you acquainted with Miss de Coverdale?'

'No. At least, not formally,' Oliver amended quickly. 'I was not aware of her name until today. But I remember seeing her…many years ago under considerably different circumstances. I was wondering how she came to be in your employ.'

Mrs Guarding walked towards a fine black lacquer desk and sat down behind it. 'Would it surprise you to learn that Miss de Coverdale was once a pupil here?'

'Yes.' Oliver picked up a particularly fine cloisonné vase from the table and turned it over in his hands. 'Am I to assume she comes from a privileged background?'

'Not privileged, but certainly genteel. Her father was a barrister. Her mother, I believe, was of foreign birth. Helen was with us for a few years and showed great promise with her drawing. And of course, she spoke Italian beautifully. After she left, I heard nothing more about her. Until three years ago when to my great surprise, I received a letter from her, asking if I would consider giving her employment as a teacher.'

'Which you agreed to do.'

'Most happily. I was delighted to have a teacher with her skills.'

Oliver nodded, pausing for a moment to deliberate upon how best to phrase his next question. 'Does she have any…gentlemen friends?'

'If she has, I am not aware of it. Miss de Coverdale seldom leaves the building.'

'Not even to visit family?'

'She has no family in England. Her parents are both dead and I have never heard her refer to anyone else in conversation.'

'I see.' Oliver crossed his arms over his chest. 'Mrs Guarding, did Miss de Coverdale provide you with suitable references when she came to you?'

He saw a brief flash of annoyance darken the headmistress's eyes. 'Of course. Have you any reason to believe she would not?'

His shrug was purposely evasive. 'I am merely curious as to the nature of Miss de Coverdale's past employment.'

Mrs Guarding abruptly rose and crossed to the bell pull. 'Miss de Coverdale's work as governess to the children of Lord and Lady Peregrine was spoken of in glowing terms. The letter was written by Lady Peregrine herself, if that is of any consequence.'

Oliver smiled faintly. He had put the headmistress on the defensive, and her message to him was quite clear. She did not care to entertain intrusive questions about her staff, nor did she feel compelled to answer them. 'I shall take up no more of your time, madam. I ask only that you provide me with periodic reports as to Gillian's progress. I have reason to believe she will experience some difficulties in settling in, but I am sure everything will be fine once she comes to know the other girls.'

'I am confident she will fit in very well, Mr Brandon. But I shall keep you apprised of her progress.' The door opened and a black-garbed maid entered. 'Molly will show you out.'

Oliver bowed. 'Thank you.'

As Oliver followed the maid down the hall, he admitted to feeling a certain degree of frustration. He was no further ahead *after* his conversation with Mrs Guarding than he had been before it. It was clear the headmistress thought well of Miss de Coverdale, and it was equally clear there was nothing in her past that would have precluded her from being taken on as a teacher here.

But how could a woman who had been employed in a household where she might well have been the lord's mistress, receive a glowing report from the lord's wife? Had she been that good at concealing the nature of her relationships? Oliver wondered. Or had she simply been fortunate enough to end up in a

household where the wife knew of her husband's behaviour, and had been equally willing to turn a blind
eye to it?

Helen set her easel close to the base of the linden
tree and checked to make sure that the footing was
secure. 'Now, girls,' she said, turning to smile at the
eight young women who were gathered around her,
'I thought today we might begin work on a new land-
scape. Miss Tillendon, did you not express the opinion that it would be challenging to paint the varying
shades of blue in the sky?'

'Yes, Miss de Coverdale.'

'Then I think that is what we shall undertake. Now,
to begin with, we should spend a little time studying
the sky. We should look up and see how the colours
in it change. Notice the way the blue is lighter there,
and how the clouds come across it and make it appear—'

'Miss de Coverdale, who is that gentleman?'
Rebecca Walters enquired suddenly.

Helen abruptly turned away from her study of the
sky to glance in the direction Rebecca was pointing.
To her astonishment, she saw Oliver Brandon striding
down the path towards them, his face set in grim
lines. He covered the distance between the school and
the pasture in short measure, but then, as if uncertain
of his welcome, stopped at the edge of the field and
leaned against the fence.

Helen felt a quick surge of colour to her cheeks.
What was Oliver Brandon doing out here? Surely he
wasn't expecting to have a conversation with her right
in the middle of her lesson? But why else would he

have come? He would hardly be interested in watching a group of young girls learn how to paint.

'The gentleman's name is Mr Brandon,' Helen said, seeing no reason not to tell them. 'He is the guardian of one of our new students, Miss Gresham.'

'But why is he watching you?' Lydia McPherson piped up.

'He isn't watching me, Miss McPherson. He is watching all of us attempt to paint the sky.'

'I think he is looking at you, Miss,' little Eliza Howard said shyly. 'He is too old to care about the rest of us, or about our paintings.'

The girls started to giggle and Helen felt the blush in her cheeks spread to the rest of her face. '*If* he is looking at me, it is only because he wishes to see how I conduct my classes. His ward is to be a pupil here. No doubt he wishes to see what kind of teacher I am.'

'I shouldn't mind his watching *me*,' Rebecca Walters said on a sigh. 'He's ever so handsome.'

Elizabeth Brookwell gave a disparaging snort. 'You think all gentlemen are handsome.'

'I do not!'

'Yes you do!'

'Ladies, please!' Helen interrupted firmly. 'It is not for us to wonder why Mr Brandon has chosen to stand by the fence and watch us. He is perfectly within his rights to do so, and I am sure it is nothing more than curiosity. Now, kindly return your attention to the sky. If you will recall, I was remarking on the number of shades of blue to be seen. Who can tell me how many different shades there are?'

The question served to focus the attention of most of the girls back on their work, and gave Helen a legitimate reason to ignore Oliver Brandon. But she could not so easily dismiss the awareness of his presence standing some thirty feet away. It was all very well to say he was only there to observe the activities of girls at their lessons. It was another thing entirely to believe it.

Oliver stood by the gate and watched Helen de Coverdale conduct an art class for the small cluster of girls gathered around her. They had each brought easels, paints and papers with them, and from what he could see, they were all diligently trying to replicate the ever-changing shades of blue in the afternoon sky. Even from this distance, however, it was obvious that most of them would never be called upon to make a living from their art. But what about the woman standing in the middle of the circle? What had happened to bring about such a change in her life?

There was no question in Oliver's mind that Helen de Coverdale was wasting her time here. With those full pouting lips and that blatantly sensual figure, she could have been one of the most sought after courtesans in London. Wealthy, aristocratic gentlemen would have vied with one another to offer her their protection, while handsome young bucks would have been lined up outside her door.

And who could blame them? Oliver had never seen such a combination of innocence and sensuality in a woman before. Her skin was itself a palette upon which an artist might sketch. But unlike canvas, it invited touch. Even from this distance, he had an overwhelming urge to run his fingers over her face and see if it felt as warm and as soft as it looked. And her movements fascinated him. Helen de

Coverdale walked amongst the girls with the same languid grace she had demonstrated in the dining-hall; her hips following her legs in a movement that was decidedly provocative, yet totally instinctual. Her attire, a simple, round gown of unadorned muslin, was not designed to flatter her figure, yet the voluptuous curves of her hips and the fullness of her breasts caused it to appear enticing in spite of it being so plain. Furthermore, in direct contrast to what was expected of a woman in her position, she did not hide her hair under a cap or restrain it in a matronly style. The glorious tresses rippled freely down her back, falling almost to her waist in a dark, shimmering stream.

Yes, she was certainly a woman to be desired, Oliver acknowledged. And given what he had seen of her conduct in the library at Grovesend Hall, she was not inexperienced in the arts of love. But if that was the case, what was she doing here? Sophie had assured him that the teachers at the Guarding Academy were all of the highest moral character. Yet what he had witnessed of Helen de Coverdale's conduct in the past had been impropriety, plain and simple. How could a woman like that be hired to teach moral rectitude to the young women in her care?

Suddenly, Oliver straightened. The lady in question had broken away from her girls and was walking towards him.

Without thinking, he pushed himself away from the gate and removed his beaver. She might be a lightskirt, but she was a woman, and his manners were too deeply ingrained to allow him to treat her any differently. Besides, to demonstrate such shocking lack of manners in front of a group of young girls who were even now casting secretive glances in their direction would have been the height of rudeness.

Nevertheless, Oliver kept his voice polite but cool as he sketched her a brief bow. 'Good afternoon, Miss de Coverdale. I hope my study has not disturbed you.'

'It has not disturbed *me*, Mr Brandon, but I fear you are affecting the concentration of some of my girls,' Helen said quietly. 'They are easily distracted by the presence of strangers, especially those about whom they are curious.'

Oliver had expected her voice to be as seductive as everything else about her, but he was surprised to discover that her eyes were not brown as he had first thought, but a most unusual shade of dark green flecked with bits of amber and gold. 'I apologise for any disruption I might be causing, Miss de Coverdale. I was simply curious to see if you were as good an artist as Mrs Guarding led me to believe.'

The beautiful eyes grew wary. 'You discussed me with Mrs Guarding?'

'Of course. As I discussed all of the teachers I met this morning. I thought it only wise since my ward is to be a pupil here.'

Oliver knew he didn't owe her an explanation, but neither did he wish to make her feel as though he had singled her out. *Why* he should be concerned with her feelings, he had no idea. After all, it was not *his* conduct that had engendered his current opinion of her.

'Does your ward like to paint?' Helen surprised him by asking.

'Paint? Yes, I suppose she does. Gillian is skilled in a number of areas, including those of a more creative nature.'

'Good. Then I look forward to the opportunity of working with her.'

'That is what I would like to speak to you about, Miss de Coverdale,' Oliver said stiffly. 'I think there are things which need to be clarified—'

Suddenly, a clattering behind them, followed by smothered gasps and then a burst of feminine giggles, brought an abrupt end to their conversation.

'Miss de Coverdale, come quickly!' one of the girls cried. 'Rebecca's easel has fallen over and she is all spattered with yellow and blue paint.'

Helen's eyes widened as she turned to survey the spectacle. 'Dear me! Miss Walters, did I not tell you to make sure your easel was securely placed?' She turned back around and Oliver was surprised to see not anger, but laughter bubbling in the depths of her beautiful eyes. 'Forgive me, Mr Brandon, I fear I must return to my class.'

'But it is important that we speak—'

'I am sure whatever you need say to me can wait, sir.'

With that, she turned and hurried back towards her class. The girls were all clustered around the unfortunate Rebecca, ineffectually dabbing their small white handkerchiefs at the spots of yellow and blue paint on her smock. Oliver listened as Helen put one of the older girls in charge, and then watched her escort the stricken Rebecca back to the school. Once again, she did not spare him a second glance.

Oliver bit back a sigh of vexation. He was not used to being summarily dismissed, and certainly not by a woman like Helen de Coverdale. But she had made her position clear. Obviously if he wished to have any

kind of private conversation with her, it was either
going to have to be before her classes, or after them.

Helen was somewhat surprised that she did not see
Oliver Brandon again that day, but she was not in the
least surprised to receive a summons to the headmistress's sitting-room later that afternoon.

'I hope you do not mind my asking you here,
Helen,' Mrs Guarding began, 'but I think you know
the reason why.'

Helen sighed. She had long since come to realise
that Eleanor Guarding was not only an intelligent
woman but an intuitive one. She had obviously seen
the look on Oliver Brandon's face this morning—as
well as on her own—and the interview now was about
achieving an understanding of what those looks had
been about. For the good of the school, of course.

'Not at all,' Helen said, taking the indicated seat in
front of the headmistress's desk. 'I am sure you noticed my reaction to Mr Brandon.'

The headmistress smiled. 'I am used to young
women blushing in the presence of a handsome gentleman, but I thought your response indicated something more than just a touch of simple embarrassment.'

Helen was dismayed to feel fresh colour rise to her
cheeks. 'It isn't what you think.'

'Oh? What is it you perceive I think it might be?'

'I am not *acquainted* with Mr Brandon,' Helen said
carefully. 'I merely saw him at the home of one of
my employers, many years ago.'

'Really. And yet it struck me there was some discomfort on your part. Why would that be, if you had
done nothing more than see him?'

'Because I saw him while I was being...' Helen broke off, finding it difficult even now to say the words. 'While I was being most...rudely treated by the man whose daughters I had been engaged to look after.'

'I see.' There was a moment's silence during which all that could be heard was the ticking of the mantel clock. Then Mrs Guarding nodded. 'It would be foolish of me to pretend an ignorance of what goes on in the world, Helen. You would not be the first woman to be unjustly put upon, and I sympathise with you for what you had to endure. I take it Mr Brandon did not realise what was happening at the time?'

'No. I am quite sure he believed he was witnessing a mutually agreeable embrace. He said nothing, but he left the room very quickly.'

'And you have not seen him since?'

'No. I left Lord Talbot's employ the very next day.'

Mrs Guarding laced her fingers together on the desk in front of her. 'Well, I think we need say no more about it. I apologise if my question seemed intrusive, but for the good of the school, I had to ask.'

'I understand.'

'My other reason for inviting you here was to inform you of Mr Brandon's concerns with regard to his ward.'

Helen frowned. 'Concerns?'

'Yes. It seems Miss Gresham has been keeping company with a gentleman by the name of Sidney Wymington. Mr Brandon is not happy with her choice of companion and has sent her here to place her beyond Mr Wymington's reach.'

Helen glanced at the headmistress in confusion.

'But if he has sent her here for that reason, why is he still concerned?'

'Because he is of the opinion that Mr Wymington may try to get in touch with Miss Gresham here. As such, he has asked me to advise my staff that she is not to receive letters from the gentleman, nor to entertain him here. She is also not to leave the school grounds unescorted.'

At the headmistress's words, Helen felt a mixture of anger and resentment kindle in her breast. Why did men always feel they had the right to meddle in other people's lives? Especially those of their wives or daughters? Oliver Brandon was interfering in his ward's life in exactly the same way her own father had meddled in hers; an interference which had cost Helen the love of the man she had dearly hoped to marry. Why was everyone so willing to accept such high-handed treatment?

'Do you agree with what he is asking you to do?' she asked stiffly.

Mrs Guarding picked up her teacup and raised it to her lips. 'It is not for me to agree or disagree, Helen. Mr Brandon's ward is my pupil; therefore, I have no choice but to act in accordance with his instructions. He has made me aware of certain facts and I must now do whatever I can to ensure that Miss Gresham and Mr Wymington do not meet.'

'But what if he is wrong about the gentleman?' Helen felt compelled to ask. 'What if Mr Wymington is a perfectly amiable man who loves Miss Gresham and who has the best of intentions at heart?'

'That possibility certainly exists, but it is not up to you or me to make it known to Mr Brandon. He has paid his ward's tuition in full and has also made a most generous donation of books. I am in no position to challenge him about what he does and does not feel is right for his ward.'

'But he is interfering in a young girl's life!'

'A young girl who is legally in his care,' the headmistress reminded her. 'As such, one who must be expected to abide by his decisions. I do hope I have your co-operation in this, Helen. I cannot have individual members of my staff acting of their own volition in matters such as these.'

Helen bit back the words she longed to speak and vented her frustration in a sigh. She knew there was only one answer she could give. Whatever her own feelings in the matter, they could have no place here. For the good of the school, she had to comply with Mrs Guarding's wishes. But not for the first time in her life, the rules by which she was forced to live sat ill upon her conscience. 'Yes, of course you have my co-operation.'

Mrs Guarding looked considerably relieved. 'Thank you. I know you have strong feelings in the matter, my dear, but we really have no choice. If we do not do as Mr Brandon asks, he will simply remove his ward and demand a refund of the tuition he has already paid. And then we shall be in forfeit of both his good opinion and his funding.'

'Yes, I know,' Helen murmured reluctantly. 'But it does not make me any the happier for knowing.'

'We must do the best we can.' Mrs Guarding smiled. 'Thank you too for telling me the truth about the manner of your first introduction to Mr Brandon.'

'Why would I not?'

'Because it is not always easy to tell people about things we are ashamed of, especially if they happened

in our distant past. And it takes even more courage
to admit them to me.'

Somewhat reluctantly, Helen began to smile. 'I had
no idea what Mr Brandon might have told you. In the
event he told you what *he* remembered seeing all
those years ago, I thought it would be in both of our
interests to tell you what *really* happened.'

'And that is why we need say no more about it.'
Mrs Guarding raised the teacup to her lips again. 'As
far as I am concerned, the matter is closed.'

Chapter Four

Perhaps because of what Mrs Guarding told her about Gillian Gresham, Helen found herself taking a keener interest in the girl than usual.

That she was resentful at having been forced to come to Guarding's was obvious. The girl attended classes but remained stubbornly uncommunicative throughout. Even when she was compelled to answer a question, she did so grudgingly and more often than not, with the very minimum of conversation required. Most of the teachers soon began to express frustration at dealing with the child, and as the end of Gillian's first week approached, Helen was more inclined to believe that Oliver Brandon had done his half sister a disservice by forcing her to come to Guarding's, rather than a good turn.

Of course, Helen knew better than most what it was like to have other people make decisions for one, especially in matters of the heart. She knew the hurt that resulted from being told that the man you loved was totally unsuitable—whether he was, in fact, or not—and she knew that because of the resentment Gillian was feeling towards Oliver, everyone else would be made to suffer too. For that reason alone, Helen knew she had to try to get closer to her. It wasn't Gillian's fault she was here. Like most women, she had very little say about what she could and could not do with her life.

'Miss Gresham, you have a very nice grasp of colour and balance in your paintings,' Helen complimented her one afternoon. 'Your use of different shadings in the greenery of the new and old leaves is very good.'

Gillian shrugged. 'I like to paint. And I paint what I see.'

'So do all the other young ladies, but they do not have as good an eye as you when it comes to colour.'

Gillian looked up at her, and for a moment her face brightened in a smile. It was a fleeting gesture, there and then gone, but it was enough to make Helen marvel at the change it wrought in the girl's appearance. Goodness, it was like the sun coming out after a summer storm. It also made her more determined than ever to break through the barrier of silence and to find out what was really going on in Gillian's mind.

Happily, the opportunity arose a few days later. Helen had taken a book out to a secluded area of the garden to read. It was one of her favourite places and she often retired there to sit and write letters, or to indulge her love of reading. It was there Gillian came upon her. 'Good afternoon, Miss de Coverdale,' she said politely.

'Good afternoon, Miss Gresham.'

'I hope I am not disturbing you, but Mrs Guarding told me I should come outside and take some fresh air.' Gillian flounced down on the seat next to her. 'She said I was looking peaky. Do you think I am?

Helen pretended to do a study of the girl's face. 'I think perhaps you are a trifle pale, but I would not say peaky.'

'That was what I thought too. I do not think anyone has ever called me peaked before.' Gillian sighed again, and then glanced at the book Helen was reading. 'Are you sure I am not disturbing you?'

'Not at all. I was just about to stop for a while anyway.' Helen closed the book and set it aside. '*Othello* is a diverting tale, but I confess I do not like it as well as some of Mr Shakespeare's other works.'

Gillian's eyes opened wide. 'Oh, but how can you not! It is so very romantic. Indeed, Mr Wymington quotes to me from it frequently.'

The mention of the notorious Mr Wymington's name did not escape Helen's notice, but she decided to ignore it for the moment. Better not to express too much curiosity this early in the game. 'Well, you have been here over a week now, Miss Gresham. What do you think of Guarding's?'

Gillian shrugged and some of the gaiety left her eyes. 'It is not as dreadful as I thought it would be. The teachers are all very nice, and so are the girls, but some of them are frightfully intelligent. Annabelle James is brilliant at maths, and Mary Putford knows how to speak French, Italian *and* Greek fluently.'

Helen arched one dark brow in surprise. 'Miss Putford is fluent in Greek? Dear me, perhaps I should ask her if she would be willing to take classes once a week.'

Gillian shrugged again. 'I expect she would. She confided to me that she would very much like to be a teacher one day.'

Helen glanced at the girl in surprise. Mary Putford

was a pleasant girl and one generally acknowledged by all as being exceedingly bright, but to the best of Helen's knowledge she seldom mixed with the other girls. How interesting to discover that in the short time Gillian had been here, she had somehow managed to get close enough to Mary to know that she both spoke Greek *and* that she was interested in teaching it.

Clearly there was more to Gillian Gresham than met the eye.

'So, does that mean you are not entirely sorry to be here with us rather than back home in Hertfordshire?' Helen enquired with a smile.

'Not entirely, though I would never tell Oliver that.' Gillian watched a small green caterpillar inch its way through the grass at her feet. 'I want him to suffer terrible feelings of guilt for having left me here. I intend to make sure he knows that if I waste away to nothing, it will all have been his fault.'

Helen was careful not to smile, though she was very much tempted to. 'I hardly think he will believe that, Miss Gresham.'

'Nor do I, but it pleases me to think he might. I would certainly not tell him that I do not miss stuffy old Shefferton Hall at all.' Gillian sighed. 'The only problem is that I *do* miss my dear Mr Wymington.'

Thinking it might sound strange if she did not enquire about a gentleman who had now been mentioned twice in conversation, Helen said, 'And who is Mr Wymington?'

Once again, the change in Gillian's appearance was remarkable. She clasped her hands together in front of her and her smile grew positively radiant. 'He is the most kind and considerate gentleman I have ever known. He is a lieutenant in the militia, and surely the most handsome man in the entire regiment!'

'Is he indeed? And is there an arrangement between the two of you?'

The girl's animation vanished like a candle being extinguished. 'I only wish there were. Oliver does not care for Mr Wymington. That is why he sent me here. He does not wish me to see him ever again.'

Helen had to exercise a certain amount of care as regards what she said next. She knew it would be wrong to encourage Gillian to go against the wishes of her guardian, but she did want to hear Gillian's side of the story. After all, it was entirely possible that Oliver Brandon's reasons for wishing to separate the two were entirely groundless. 'Why doesn't your guardian like Mr Wymington?'

'Because he thinks he is only after my money. I'm an heiress, you see, Miss de Coverdale. When I turn one-and-twenty, I shall inherit a great deal of money.'

'And is Mr Wymington in possession of a good income himself?'

'No. At least, none that he has ever mentioned to me.'

Which probably meant he wasn't, Helen reflected silently. Lower-ranking officers did not earn a great deal of money, and half-pay officers even less. 'Then it is entirely possible your guardian is right,' Helen replied, willing for the moment to give Mr Brandon the benefit of the doubt. 'It is not unheard of for young gentlemen who are in, shall we say…restricted financial circumstances to be attracted to wealthy young women,' she pointed out. 'Especially when they are as pretty as you.'

The young woman's face brightened again. 'Do you really think I am pretty?'

'Of course, but I am sure Mr Wymington has told you that.'

The blush in the girl's cheeks deepened. 'Miss de Coverdale, may I ask you a question?'

'You may.'

'It is rather personal.'

'I shan't answer it if it is too personal.'

'Well, it is just that…why would someone as beautiful as *you* not be married?'

Helen blinked her surprise. 'Good Lord. Whatever made you ask such a thing?'

'Because you are not like the other teachers here. Oh, they are all very pleasant, to be sure, but none of them are anywhere near as lovely as you. And I know that gentlemen are attracted to pretty ladies. So I simply wondered why you were not married.'

'Perhaps no one has ever asked me,' Helen said in as light-hearted a tone as she could manage.

'But you have been in love, haven't you?'

Oh yes, I have been in love, Helen thought wistfully. *But like your guardian, my father did not approve of the gentleman I loved either, and he had him sent away too.*

'I think it would be best if we were to talk about your hopes for the future, Miss Gresham, rather than sit here and discuss something which is of no importance to either of us.'

'But love *is* important,' Gillian said desperately. 'Surely it is the most important thing in the world!'

'It is important, to be sure,' Helen agreed, 'but there are many things which take precedence over it.

Like the value of a good education, for example, which is why you are here.'

Gillian snorted. 'I am here because Oliver does not wish me to see Mr Wymington and because there was nowhere else he could send me.'

There was an unknowingly wistful note to the girl's voice and it tugged at Helen's heart. 'I am sure your guardian only has your interests at heart, Miss Gresham. He is older than you, and he knows what is best.'

'But how can he know what is best when he has never been in love?' Gillian cried in frustration. 'How can he know…how sweet it is to be close to someone you love when he has never experienced those feelings himself?'

Helen blinked in surprise. A gentleman as handsome as Oliver Brandon had never fallen victim to love? How very strange. 'Are you sure he has never felt that way?'

'Oh yes. I have spent most of my life in Oliver's house, and I know him better than anyone. Except perhaps his sister, but even Sophie knows what it's like to be in love.'

'Is she a married lady?'

'Yes, and a most happy one. I like her very much. We have the most interesting talks, even though she is very sensible.'

Helen hid her smile, amused by the notion that in Gillian's mind, being sensible *and* being interesting were not necessarily synonymous. 'What does she say about your association with Mr Wymington?'

'She doesn't say very much at all,' Gillian admitted. 'But then she hardly would, being Oliver's sister. She would never express an opinion contrary to his.'

'Has she met Mr Wymington?' Helen enquired.

'Once. I introduced them at a musicale.'

'And did she appear to like him?'

Gillian frowned. 'I do not know. I cannot recall her saying very much about him at the time.'

'But she did spend enough time in his company to form an opinion of him?'

'Oh yes. Sophie is very good at forming opinions of other people. And she is seldom wrong.'

'Then, if she is good at judging other people's characters, and she is seldom wrong, why would she not tell Mr Brandon he had made an error in judgement with regard to Mr Wymington if she truly believed he had?'

It was a neatly worded exercise that forced Gillian to acknowledge the fact that a woman she considered eminently sensible had made her own decision regarding Mr Wymington and that it might be less than favourable. Unfortunately, Helen could also tell from the look on Gillian's face that she was not about to concede the point so easily.

'Sophie is very capable of forming her own opinions, but she is not always given to sharing them. But I do not believe she would tell me she liked Mr Wymington if she knew her brother would object.'

This time, Helen decided to let it go. She had a sneaking suspicion that Oliver's sister did *not* approve of Mr Wymington and that Gillian was perfectly well aware of it. But her reluctance to admit it naturally begged the question why?

What was there about the dashing young gentleman that both Oliver *and* his happily married sister could object to?

* * *

Oliver read the letter from Gillian, the third he'd received since he'd left her at Guarding's, and frowned in consternation.

> Miss de Coverdale has such a refreshing outlook on everything, Oliver. Indeed, I almost feel as though I am talking to someone my own age, rather than someone closer to yours...

Oliver sighed. Obviously she thought him quite decrepit.

> Miss de Coverdale...Helen as I like to think of her...has also told me about the scandalous events which have taken place in Steep Abbot. It seems the old Marquis was murdered right here in the Abbey and that everyone has a different opinion as to who did it.
>
> Many believe it was his wife, while others say it was his faithful servant. Really, Oliver, it is quite fascinating. The girls talk about it incessantly...

Oliver threw down the letter and began to pace. Wonderful. Not only was his ward forming a close friendship with a woman of questionable morals, but she was gossiping with her about the scandalous goings-on in the village where she lived. Where was the high moral fibre Sophie had spoken of in reference to the teachers at Mrs Guarding's excellent academy?

Still, he supposed gossiping about a society murder should be the least of his concerns. Far more troubling was the fact that Gillian and Miss de Coverdale were spending so much time together, and that *Helen* had such a *refreshing* outlook on everything. What was he to make of that? Was the woman encouraging Gillian in her foolish notions? Was she suggesting that his silly young ward follow her heart and act in a manner Miss de Coverdale might herself have thought appropriate at that age?

It was enough to set Oliver ringing for his valet. He did not like what he was hearing at all. He had not sent Gillian to the Guarding Academy to be corrupted by a woman like Helen de Coverdale. He *knew* he should have said something to the headmistress that first day. He should have voiced his concerns about Miss de Coverdale's past and taken pains to ensure that Gillian was not exposed to her influence. In fact, he should have stayed and *spoken* to the young woman himself instead of allowing his conscience to be assuaged by Mrs Guarding as regards the lady's character.

And that's what he was going to do now. The only way he could find out what was going on in Steep Abbot was to return there and see with his own eyes precisely what effect Helen de Coverdale was having on his ward—before any more damage was done!

Helen didn't know whether to be flattered or flummoxed by the letter she had just received. It was from Oliver Brandon, and it requested the pleasure of her company on a drive with him that very afternoon, if she could spare him the time.

Helen thoughtfully tapped the parchment against her bottom lip. As it happened, she did have some free time, given that it was her weekly half-day, but she had not thought to spend it with Mr Brandon. She had expected him to ask for a meeting to discuss the incident that had happened in her past well before now. Gillian had been at Guarding's nearly two and a half weeks. Why was he bothering to spend time with her at this late date?

Helen frowned as she put the letter on her desk. Was it possible the visit had something to do with Gillian herself? Was he concerned, perhaps, as to how well she was settling in, or as to how competent she was in her studies? Helen knew that Gillian wrote frequently to her guardian. Was it possible she had expressed unhappiness or dissatisfaction with the school, and that he was coming to see to the matter himself?

As quickly as the thought came, Helen dismissed it. No. If Mr Brandon was curious to know how his ward was progressing, he would have written to Mrs Guarding directly. The headmistress was kept fully apprised of the progress of each girl, just in case such an enquiry might arise.

Then what else could it be? Had Gillian taken a personal dislike to her and written to Mr Brandon about that? Helen didn't think so. In fact, she was rather pleased with the friendship that had sprung up between them, and she was sure it had contributed to Gillian's adapting more easily to her new environment. Even the other teachers were commenting about her sudden willingness to participate in class, and about how quick Gillian was to help the younger girls with their problems.

So if it wasn't an interrogation about her past, and it wasn't in response to a complaint from Gillian, what could Mr Brandon possibly be coming to see her about?

At precisely twenty-seven minutes past three, Helen closed the door to her room and walked briskly toward the stairs. The soles of her worn leather boots made a soft clicking sound against the wooden floor, but she barely heard it over the thudding of her heart. She had tried to tell herself she had nothing to worry about, but after much deliberation, she had concluded that the reason Mr Brandon wanted to see her today was to talk to her about her past. It was the only logical explanation.

But in recognising that, Helen also recognised that Oliver Brandon was *entitled* to know what had happened. And she felt sure that once she told him the truth—embarrassing as that might be—everything would be fine. After all, Oliver Brandon was a gentleman. As a gentleman he would understand.

He was already waiting in the hall by the time Helen descended. He looked extremely dashing this afternoon, wearing a multi-layered greatcoat over a dark jacket and light-coloured breeches. He seemed to her even larger than usual, and with his hair somewhat dishevelled by the wind, there was a roguishness about him that Helen found distinctly attractive.

She made a show of attending to her gloves, not wanting him to see how affected she really was. 'Good afternoon, Mr Brandon. I hope I have not kept you waiting.'

Oliver turned at the sound of her voice and sketched her a perfunctory bow. 'On the contrary, Miss de Coverdale, you are exceedingly punctual.'

The formal tone gave Helen a moment's pause, but she told herself to ignore it. It was only natural that his speech would be short. No doubt his impressions of her prevented him from being anything but distant.

In the courtyard, a stylish curricle drawn by two perfectly matched blacks awaited their arrival.

'Oh, what a splendid pair,' Helen commented with approval. 'Do they go as sweetly as they look?'

'They do indeed. Are you at skilled at tooling the ribbons, Miss de Coverdale?'

'I used to be,' Helen admitted as he settled her into the passenger seat, 'but a great deal of time has passed since then, and I should not like to comment upon my abilities now.'

'It is not something one forgets,' Mr Brandon observed, climbing up beside her.

'No, but neither is it a skill which improves with lack of practice. However, on such a lovely day as this, I am quite content to sit back and enjoy someone else's skill.'

And truly, it was a perfect mid-September day. The slight briskness in the air encouraged the wearing of gloves and a light coat, but it was not so cold as to be uncomfortable. Helen wished she might have had a prettier gown to wear, but such things were not available to a young woman in her position. The dark green spencer over the plain cambric gown did very well, as did her poke-bonnet tied with a matching ribbon. The newest thing she owned was a pair of buttery-soft kid gloves, a much-cherished Christmas present from her friend Desirée.

Mr Brandon gathered up the reins and set the pair to a brisk trot. His hands were firm but never harsh on the reins, and Helen enjoyed watching him employ his skills at keeping the pair to a steady trot. She also liked the fact that he seldom used the whip. She had seen far too many young men try to demonstrate their skill with the tool, only to have the horses suffer for their inadequacy. But when Mr Brandon employed the whip, it was with such a light hand that Helen knew it was the sound of the snap more than the touch that set the horses to responding. Besides, with a pair of high-steppers like these, it would hardly be necessary.

They drove for a few miles in silence, enjoying the loveliness of the autumn day. Helen wished she could have said she was enjoying Oliver's company as much, but with every minute that passed, her feelings of apprehension grew. The knowledge that she was going to have to talk about an incident which had caused her so much pain and embarrassment was not conducive to serenity.

Finally, when she could bear the silence no longer, she turned to him with the question on her lips. To her surprise, she was forestalled by one of his.

'Where did you learn to speak Italian, Miss de Coverdale?'

Helen blinked. 'I…beg your pardon?'

'Italian.' Oliver favoured her with a piercing gaze. 'It is an unusual language for an Englishwoman to be teaching, is it not?'

'Well, no, not…really,' Helen stammered. 'My mother was Italian.'

'But not your father.'

'No. He was English. My mother met him while she was visiting friends in Canterbury. They married soon after.'

'Did they return to Italy?'

Helen shook her head. 'My father was already established in England so there was no question of their living abroad.'

'And was your mother happy to leave Italy?'

Helen's eyes softened. 'I don't think she was ever truly happy in England. She hated the dampness of the weather and the persistently grey skies. And I know she missed her family very much. She was one of eight children.'

'Good God, eight?'

Helen smiled. 'Italians are known for having large families. Unfortunately, my father had no desire even to visit Italy, so in the end, my mother decided to spend her summers there. And she took me with her.'

'Your father didn't mind?'

Helen shrugged. 'Theirs was an unusual marriage. My father was passionately in love with my mother, and there was nothing he could deny her. So the separations were allowed as long as they did not extend beyond a month.'

'And did *you* like Italy, Miss de Coverdale?'

'I loved it,' Helen said, with, for the first time in his company, a complete lack of reserve. 'The bright, sunny days were such a welcome change from the dreary English winters, and I found the people very open and spontaneous.'

'And that was where you learned to speak the language,' he said, making it a statement of fact rather than a question.

'Yes. My entire family conversed in Italian, so it was only natural that I would pick it up. But even when we were back in England, my mother continued to speak to me in the language. Never when my father was around, of course, but he was away so much of the time, it wasn't a problem.'

'Your father objected to you and your mother speaking in her native tongue?'

'My father thought it was rude to speak in a lan-

guage that only two of the three people in the room
could understand,' Helen told him. 'However, my
mother was of the opinion that one must use a language to stay conversant in it.'

'Just as one must practise driving to keep one's
skills up,' Oliver said distantly.

Helen flashed him an amused glance. 'Just so.'

They drove on again in silence. A few other car-
riages passed them, but for the most part, they had
the road to themselves. Helen didn't even trouble to
hide her pleasure at being driven out on such a beautiful day. She even endeavoured to make light conversation about some of the places they passed, but
as her attempts were often met with silence she soon
gave up.

Finally, when the silence again became uncomfortable, she took a long, deep breath and turned to
face him. 'Mr Brandon, I must confess to a certain…surprise at having received your letter. It is
most unusual for a schoolmistress to spend time alone
with the parent of one of her girls.'

'I seldom trouble myself with what is or is not
usual, Miss de Coverdale,' Oliver replied blandly. 'I
wished to speak to you alone and perceived this to be
the best way of doing that.'

'But…what did you wish to speak to me about?'

Oliver sent her a mocking glance. 'Do you really
need ask, given the nature of our first acquaintance?'

Helen quickly averted her eyes. So, it was as she
had expected. 'I see. You wish to ask me about…
what you saw in the library that night.'

'Yes, but only as it affects your relationship with
my ward.'

'I beg your pardon?'

'I will be honest, Miss de Coverdale. I might not have found this interview necessary had Gillian's letters to me not been filled with such glowing praise about *you*.'

Helen's eyes opened wide. 'She wrote to you about me?'

'Frequently. And in the most flattering of terms.' When she made no answer, Oliver's lips curved in a sardonic smile. 'You seem surprised, Miss de Coverdale. Did you not expect Gillian to speak well of you?'

'I had no idea how she would speak of me. I thought we had established a friendship, but I...'

'Yes?'

Biting her lip, Helen looked away. 'If your ward thinks well of me and has written to tell you as much, why did you feel it necessary to speak to me about...something of which she has no knowledge?'

'Because it is not Gillian's ignorance of the event which concerns me,' Oliver informed her. 'She told me you had a *refreshing* outlook toward certain subjects. I am simply curious to know which subjects those might be.'

Frowning, Helen shook her head. 'I cannot honestly say, sir. We talk of so many things it is difficult to remember the nature of every conversation.'

'Then let me see if I can narrow the field somewhat. Did Mrs Guarding apprise you of a situation with regard to a Mr Sidney Wymington?'

Helen grew wary. 'Yes.'

'And has my ward also made mention of that gentleman?'

Knowing there was no point in denying it, Helen inclined her head. 'Yes, she has.'

'Then I'm sure you can understand why I might wish to speak with you in private regarding the matter.'

Helen's brow furrowed. 'In truth, sir, I cannot. Unless you have some reason to believe I would not adhere to your wishes.'

'Miss de Coverdale, let us not mince words. I saw you in the library with Lord Talbot. I know you were not there to discuss the merits of literature and given that knowledge, I think you can understand why I was so surprised at finding you here, acting out the part of schoolmistress.'

An angry flush suffused Helen's face. 'I do not *act* the part, sir. I *am* a teacher and I take great pride in what I do. Have you reason to doubt my abilities?'

'Not at all. Mrs Guarding spoke most highly of your skills.'

'Then I do not understand—'

'The issue I wished to address, Miss de Coverdale, is one of morality, not proficiency.'

'Morality!'

'Yes. Since you are aware of my feelings with regard to Mr Wymington, I am sure you can understand why I would be concerned about any…influence you might have on Gillian in regard to that situation.'

'I do not understand your concerns at all,' Helen replied, her voice curt. 'If you do not wish your ward to have anything to do with the man, what makes you think I would?'

'Because given your behaviour in the past, I am not sure you have as high a moral character as I would like.'

His words struck her like a slap across the face and Helen swallowed hard, fighting to keep her composure. 'Mr Brandon, I understand how you might have been tempted to form certain…opinions of me based upon what you saw. But to still hold me in such contempt for a perceived indiscretion twelve years later demonstrates to my way of thinking a shocking narrowness of mind.'

'Narrowness of mind!'

'Indeed, sir. You formed an impression of my character based upon what you thought you saw—'

'Based upon what I *did* see.'

'No, sir. Based upon what you *thought* you saw, and have held it to this day, without even giving me a chance to explain.'

'Then explain yourself now,' Oliver snapped. 'You have not once tried to deny that you *were* the woman I saw in Lord Talbot's arms that night.'

'No, because it would be foolish of me to try,' Helen flung at him. 'We both know it was me, but what you do not understand is that I was not there of my own accord.'

'Were you a servant in his house?'

'I was the governess.'

'And had Lord Talbot *asked* you to come to the library?'

'Of course not, but—'

'Then why, as a servant in the house, were you in the master's library with your hair unbound at that time of night, when you had no reason or permission to be there?'

Helen's cheeks burned. 'I had gone to procure a book. And I frequently wear my hair unbound.'

The expression on Oliver's face was not encouraging. 'Miss de Coverdale, I can find nothing in what you have just told me to justify your conduct or to make me change my opinion of you. If you felt no compunction about behaving in such a fashion, how do I know you would not counsel an impressionable young woman to do the same? Or in this case, to take up with a man I have refused to let her see!'

Oliver had not raised his voice, but the condescension in his words cut Helen to the bone. Not only was he accusing her of having behaved in a wanton and disgraceful manner, he was saying she was quite capable of persuading Gillian to do the same. He was insinuating that her character had not improved at all in the past twelve years, and that he was perfectly within his rights to believe that his assessment of her was still correct today.

And Helen resented that. She resented the implication that she was not worthy to keep company with his ward. She resented his belief that what he had witnessed twelve years ago had been the truth, even when she had tried to tell him it was not. And most deeply of all, she resented *him* for having brought it all back; for making her relive the feelings of shame and degradation she had felt on that dreadful night. Feelings she had fought so long and so hard to overcome.

'Mr Brandon, I do not think there is anything else which needs to be said between us,' Helen said, finally turning to look at him. 'Obviously the testimonials of people who know me far better than you, and who are willing to vouch for my respectability, mean nothing, so I would ask you to be so good as to take me back to Guarding's.'

Oliver reined the team in, but he did not turn the carriage around. 'I do not understand why you evidence such surprise at my comment, Miss de

Coverdale. I was a witness to what took place in the library at Grovesend Hall, not the cause of it.'

'Nor was I, Mr Brandon, but since you obviously aren't willing to believe that, I do not see that we have anything further to discuss.'

'Miss de Coverdale—'

'For the last time, sir, would you please take me home,' Helen said stiffly. 'I have done nothing to deserve such treatment from you, and unless you have an apology to offer, there is nothing more I wish to hear.'

Oliver had no intention of offering an apology, and as if finally realising that Helen had indeed, no intention of speaking another word to him, he cursed softly and turned the team around. He flicked the reins and set them to a brisk trot.

Not another word was spoken the entire way home.

Chapter Five

Helen decided not to tell Gillian she had driven out with her guardian. After all, what would be the point? Nothing would be gained by such an admission. Gillian would want to know the details of what they had talked about, and Helen had no intention of telling her. Yes, there was a chance Gillian might find out about the meeting and then accuse Helen of holding something back, but it was a slim chance at best. Gillian certainly wouldn't hear the truth from her stepbrother. Why would he bring up a subject that would expose him to a barrage of questions he would be no more anxious to answer than Helen?

Thankfully, the subject did not arise, and when Helen heard from Gillian that Oliver had been called away to London on business, she could not find it in her heart to be sorry. The man had insulted her in every possible way. He had all but called her a trollop, and then accused her of corrupting the innocents in her care.

Was it any wonder his company was something Helen was all too happy to avoid?

* * *

Sunday mornings were typically reserved for service in Abbot Quincey, and at nine o'clock Helen and Gillian set off for church. They were accompanied by three of the other teachers, Jane Emerson, Ghislaine de Champlain and Henriette Mason, as well as by a few of the girls. Mr and Mrs Guarding always took the youngest ones in their carriage, but the older pupils and the teachers were quite happy to walk. It afforded them an opportunity to enjoy the beauty of the countryside, and to escape, if only for a few hours, the somewhat confining atmosphere of the school.

Abbot Quincey was the largest of the four Abbey villages. It boasted a fine old church, the living of which was held by the Reverend William Perceval, a kindly man with a wife and four daughters, and a younger brother to Lord Perceval. Helen had always enjoyed the Reverend Perceval's sermons. In the quiet of the village church, and in the companionship of her friends, she experienced a sense of peace and contentment as the gentle words of forgiveness flowed all around her. Unfortunately, on this particular morning, Helen found little to take comfort in. The memory of Oliver Brandon's visit and the disturbing things he had said to her stayed with her the entire time, intruding painfully into the serenity of her thoughts.

Fortunately, not everyone was as disconsolate as she. Jane Emerson sat quietly beside her on one side of the wooden pew and Gillian sat on the other, the girl's gloved hands folded primly in her lap as she listened to the words of the sermon. It was a particularly moving lesson on the value of patience and the importance of forgiveness in everyday life.

Helen was quite sure Oliver Brandon had never heard that particular sermon before.

As Gillian continued to sit quietly through the service, Helen found herself envying the girl's placid air of repose. How lucky she was to be seventeen and still so innocent to the ways of the world. There were no ghosts lurking in her past. No disturbing memories ready to haunt her at the slightest provocation. There was nothing anyone could say that would humiliate Gillian the way Oliver Brandon had humiliated her.

Helen sighed as she ran her gloved finger along the spine of her prayer book. Of course, she supposed he wasn't entirely to blame for what had happened between them. She should have told him *exactly* what had happened in the library with Lord Talbot. She should have *forced* him to listen and to make him understand that she had *not* been there of her own volition. But the truth was, she had been so shocked by his heartless accusation that she had been left completely at a loss for words. Indeed, she had been nearly speechless with anger.

How dare he infer that she was corrupt and immoral! He, who knew nothing of her character or her circumstances. Surely his own narrow-mindedness was every bit as grievous a flaw. After all, *she* was the one who had been willing to be conciliatory. She had even been willing to risk a scold for having been foolish enough to put herself in such an ignominious position to begin with. But she was *not* willing to be labelled a scarlet woman. If that was the make-up of the man, she was better off having nothing more to do with him. Gillian too, was better off away from such bigotry.

At length the service came to an end and people began to get up and move about. Helen rose along with the others and filed out of the church, blinking

a little as she stepped into the bright sunshine. There
were no formal classes at Guarding's on Sunday afternoons, but the girls were expected to return there
for the midday meal. After that, they could go to their
rooms, or to the common area where they might apply
themselves to their embroidery or their scriptures.
Sunday evenings were generally reserved for the reading of psalms by Mrs Guarding, and if she was so
inclined, a discussion of the sermon given by
Reverend Perceval that morning.

Helen stopped briefly to have a word with the vicar
and his wife, while Gillian struck up a conversation
with a young woman from the village. Indeed, so an-
imated was their discussion that, when it finally came
time to leave, Helen had to call Gillian away. It was
only on their way back to Steep Abbot that she discovered the reason for the girl's excitement.

'Miss de Coverdale, who do you think murdered
the old Marquis of Sywell?'

Helen caught her breath in dismay. 'Good heavens,
Miss Gresham, I have no idea. Nor do I think it a
suitable topic for us to be discussing after church on
a Sunday morning.'

'But everyone else is talking about it!' Gillian
cried. 'Imagine being murdered in your own bedroom. Apparently the murder weapon was his own
razor and there was heaps of blood everywhere! That
would be quite a shock to whoever found him, don't
you think?'

'I think it would be very shocking indeed,' Helen
allowed, knowing that the thought had crossed her
own mind several times.

'Frances Templeton thinks one of the girls who
worked as an upstairs maid murdered him,' Gillian

said. 'She said Sywell was wretched to her, as he was
to all of the servants. Personally, I am more inclined
to believe it was his wife. After all, she would have
inherited everything upon his death, wouldn't she? Or
so she would have thought.' Gillian didn't even
bother waiting for a reply. 'Louise wouldn't have
known when she murdered her husband that the
Abbey wasn't really his. But given her *belief* that it
was, and that she would inherit, I think that would
have been reason enough for her to do it, don't you?'

'I am really not acquainted with the details of the
story, Miss Gresham,' Helen said, hoping the Lord
would forgive her for the lie. Everyone knew it was
all but impossible to live this close to the Abbey and
not be aware of all the rumours and speculation going
on about its former occupant. But that was still no
reason to encourage an impressionable young woman
like Gillian to gossip about it.

'Oh, bother,' Gillian said, clearly disappointed. 'I
find the whole subject fascinating. I mean, when you
think about it, there are an endless number of people
who could have murdered him, and for any number
of reasons!'

'Which is why it would be foolish of us to attempt
a discussion of the subject,' Helen said in a firm
voice. 'Certainly we cannot do so with any degree of
intelligence. Not that murder has anything to do with
intelligence, but I think that on such a beautiful day
as this, we should be able to find something more
pleasant to talk about.'

'Oh, very well.' Gillian was silent for a moment.
'What do you think of my guardian?'

Helen all but stumbled. 'I *beg* your pardon?'

'I asked you what you thought of Oliver.'

'I know *what* you asked, Miss Gresham. I am simply wondering *why* you asked it.'

'Well, he is very handsome, don't you think?'

The abrupt switch to a topic Helen found even more disturbing than the murder at Steepwood Abbey left her feeling somewhat shaken. 'I have not given it any consideration at all. After all, the only time I've spent with Mr Brandon was on the morning you arrived,' she said, sending up another prayer for forgiveness.

'And when he came to take you driving.'

Helen came to an abrupt halt. 'How did you know about that?'

'Elizabeth Brookwell saw the two of you drive off together. Oh you needn't worry, I am not going to give you a scold,' Gillian assured her. 'I admit, I was a little put out that you didn't tell me, but then I realised you were probably just waiting for the right time to bring it up. Otherwise, I would be just as like to believe you were trying to hide something.'

Botheration, Helen thought. She should have realised that *someone* would have seen them drive off. 'I can assure you I have nothing to hide. The outing was not motivated by any feelings of personal affection on your stepbrother's part.'

'Then why did he take you driving?'

Helen started walking again. 'He wished to speak to me about something.'

'About me?'

'Partly.'

'And what else?'

'About matters which do not concern you.'

'Were they matters which concerned you?'

'Gillian, it is impolite to ask so many questions.'

'I know, but you won't give me answers otherwise. Oliver really is very nice, you know,' Gillian said, her enthusiasm not in the least dampened by the rebuke. 'Oh, I know he comes across as being terribly serious, but he isn't that way all the time. I've heard him laugh with Sophie quite often—'

'I am not interested in who Mr Brandon laughs with—'

'He drives very well too, do you not think? I don't know any other gentleman who handles a pair as well as Oliver. And he is a superb hunter.'

'Miss Gresham, why are you telling me all this?'

'Because I think the two of you would make a splendid match.'

That all but caused Helen's knees to buckle. *Herself and Oliver Brandon?* It did not even bear thinking about. 'I would thank you not to make such ridiculous suggestions, Miss Gresham. I am not looking for a husband—'

'But if you were—'

'If I were, I would still not consider Mr Brandon. We have absolutely nothing in common.'

'He thinks you're beautiful.'

Helen opened her mouth to answer, and then abruptly closed it again. No. She was not about to attempt a response to a comment like that. Apart from the fact that she was not at all sure Gillian hadn't made it up, it could have absolutely no bearing on the situation. Oliver Brandon had already told her what he thought of her. And given her knowledge of what he'd said, the fact that he thought her beautiful—if indeed he did—made for a very shallow compliment indeed.

Unfortunately, Gillian's questions and revelations

about her guardian were not the only shocks Helen
was to receive that afternoon. Just before they reached
the school gates, they heard the sound of a carriage
coming up behind them. Perpetually curious, Gillian
turned around to look, but Helen, assuming it was the
Guardings returning home, merely moved to the side
of the road.

She couldn't have been more wrong. As the equi-
page drew to a halt beside them, Gillian's startled
exclamation caused Helen to stop and whirl around.

'Oh, my dear Miss de Coverdale,' Gillian whispered in tones of barely concealed delight. 'I vow the
angels have heard my prayers! Only look! Here is
none other than my dear Mr Wymington come to pay
me a visit!'

Chapter Six

Helen could only stare in horror at the gentleman pulling the carriage to a halt beside them. *Mr Wymington?* Dear Lord, what was she to do? The one man she had been warned to keep Gillian away from was the very one who had found them! What would Mr Brandon say if he were to learn of this?

'Miss Gresham, we must continue towards the school!' Helen whispered urgently. 'You know this meeting cannot take place!'

Unfortunately, Gillian was lost to everyone but her beloved Mr Wymington. She stared at him like one in a dream, her lips parted, her eyes glowing with happiness as he jumped down from the seat and began to walk towards them. And as much as Helen might like to deny it, she could not find it in her heart to blame Gillian. The young man walking towards them was truly the embodiment of the romantic hero. Standing tall and dashing in his regimentals, with a shock of golden blond hair and eyes that were as blue as the summer's sky, he was easily one of the most handsome men Helen had ever seen.

'Mr Wymington!' Gillian cried, pouring her heart into the expression of his name.

The gentleman looked similarly elated at finding the object of his affection so close at hand and quickened his pace, causing a swath of wavy, blond hair to fall across his forehead. His smile, which had been somewhat tentative at first, widened to an expression of such heart-shattering beauty that Helen knew there was absolutely nothing she could do to prevent the meeting from taking place. However, knowing she must do whatever she could to make it as brief and as harmless as possible, she stepped in front of Gillian, placed the girl securely behind her, and addressed the man in a clear and no nonsense voice.

'Good afternoon, Mr Wymington. My name is Helen de Coverdale. I am a teacher at the Guarding Academy for Girls.'

Mr Wymington looked at Helen and offered her the same dazzling smile he had just given Gillian. 'Miss de Coverdale, I am genuinely delighted to make your acquaintance. And I feel compelled to say this is truly the most incredible of coincidences. I knew Miss Gresham was attending school near Steep Abbot, but it never crossed my mind that I would be fortunate enough to see her here.'

'But is it not wonderful that you have!' Gillian cried breathlessly.

Helen saw nothing wonderful in it at all. 'It is coincidental indeed, but what has brought you all the way from Hertfordshire on a Sunday, sir?'

'Do not fear, my reasons are entirely justified. I have come to visit my sick uncle.'

'Your uncle?' Gillian's delicate eyebrows shot upwards in surprise. 'You did not tell me you had an uncle residing in the area.'

'Indeed, I think I may have neglected to mention it,' Mr Wymington said somewhat sheepishly. 'But I do in fact have one. He lives just outside Abbot Quincey.'

'But we were just *in* Abbot Quincey,' Gillian said, her face alight with joy. 'Is that not the most amazing coincidence, Miss de Coverdale?'

'Amazing indeed,' Helen muttered, feeling it was all far *too* coincidental for her liking. 'But I'm afraid we cannot linger, Mr Wymington. We are expected back at school. If you will excuse us—'

'Oh, but why must we leave so soon?' Gillian turned to her in dismay. 'Mr Wymington has come all this way to see me—'

'To see his uncle,' Helen reminded her.

'Oh. Well, whatever the reason, he is here now. Even better, he has had a chance to meet you.'

The gentleman bowed graciously. 'I consider myself most fortunate to have had the pleasure of meeting *two* such beautiful ladies.' He glanced at Helen with unfeigned interest. 'What subjects do you teach, Miss de Coverdale?'

'Italian and watercolours,' Gillian offered impulsively. 'And she is very good at both.'

A swift rush of colour stained Helen's cheeks. 'Miss Gresham is prone to exaggeration, sir.'

'In some areas, perhaps, but not in this I shouldn't think. Otherwise you would not be employed at such a reputable establishment.'

Helen glanced at him in surprise. 'You are familiar with Mrs Guarding's Academy, Mr Wymington?'

If Helen had thought to catch him out, his answers

were to come as a disappointment. The man was no
fool. He proceeded to tell her when the school had
been established and who the headmistress was, then
further surprised her by expressing familiarity with
some of the papers Mrs Guarding had published, as
well as a knowledge of her beliefs and of the precepts
upon which the school had been founded.

For a moment, Helen could understand Gillian's
attraction to him. But she could not shake the feeling
that the meeting had been far from coincidental. 'How
long do you intend to stay in Abbot Quincey, Mr
Wymington?' she enquired.

'That depends entirely upon my uncle. He is not in
the best of health, which is why I have come to see
him. But I cannot say how long he will wish me to
stay.' Mr Wymington's expression turned endearingly
humble. 'He is a very independent gentleman and I
shouldn't wonder that he'll try to send me back to
London just as soon as he can, with the assurance that
he is quite capable of looking after himself.'

'If I were ill, I know I should very much like to
have you taking care of me,' Gillian said impulsively.

Helen only just managed not to gasp. 'I'm sorry,
Mr Wymington, but we really must be on our way.'

'Of course. It was most inconsiderate of me to de-
tain you. But I cannot deny that I have enjoyed meeting the two of you.' He smiled at them and bowed.
'Your servant, Miss de Coverdale. Miss Gresham. I
hope I shall have the honour of seeing you both again
in the near future.'

Gillian nodded fervently. 'Oh yes, we must arrange—'

'Good afternoon, Mr Wymington,' Helen said, before Gillian had time to commit any further indiscretions.

Tipping his hat, Mr Wymington returned to his carriage and headed back in the direction from whence he had come. Gillian watched the carriage until it rounded a corner and disappeared from sight. Only then did she let out a long, ecstatic sigh. 'Oh, is he not the most handsome of gentlemen, Miss de Coverdale? Indeed, he appears even more handsome to me than he did when last I saw him. Do you think it is possible for someone to grow even more handsome in the space of three weeks?'

'I very much doubt it,' Helen muttered, far less pleased with the outcome of the day than Gillian was.

'But you cannot disagree that he is handsome. Or that he is charming! Did you not think so?'

'His manners were all that were pleasing, yes.'

'Then why were you so abrupt with him?'

Helen turned and starting walking briskly in the direction of the school. 'I was not abrupt.'

'Yes, you were. I know you, Miss de Coverdale, and I know when you are being abrupt.'

'If I was short with Mr Wymington, it was only because I was not pleased at finding him here. Nor will your guardian be when he finds out.'

Gillian's face went white. 'Oh, but he mustn't find out! You mustn't tell him! If Oliver were to learn that Mr Wymington was here, there is no telling what he might do.'

'I cannot keep secrets from your guardian, Miss Gresham. Especially about this.'

'But you heard what Mr Wymington said. He came to visit his sick uncle.' Gillian scurried to keep up with her. 'Surely you cannot hold such noble motives against him.'

'I do not hold them against him. I am merely suspicious of his timing. Do you not find it disturbing that Mr Wymington suddenly decided to visit a sick uncle who just happens to live in Abbot Quincey, when he never even mentioned the *existence* of the man to you before?'

'What I find disturbing is that you are starting to sound like Oliver. Why is everyone so suspicious of Mr Wymington? Why can't anyone believe that the man is attracted to me and not to my money?'

Oh, Gillian, there is so much you need to learn, Helen thought sadly. *And we are only trying to prevent you from learning it the hard way.*

'Miss Gresham, whatever your own feelings with regard to Mr Wymington, you cannot ignore the fact that your guardian wishes you to have nothing to do with him.'

'But he has no right—'

'He has every right. Mr Brandon has let it be known that you are not to see Mr Wymington, or to correspond with him.'

'But that is not fair! Mr Wymington has done nothing wrong. Oliver doesn't like him because he reads Shakespeare to me and tells me I am pretty. What is wrong with that? Is that not the way two people who care about each other express their thoughts and feelings?'

Helen abruptly came to a halt. 'Miss Gresham—'

'Oh, do call me Gillian. At least when we are alone.'

'Very well, Gillian. You have to understand that Mr Brandon—'

'Oliver.'

'That Mr Brandon is concerned with your welfare. Many young women are taken in by a gentleman's blandishments and marry against their parents' wishes, only to come to regret it later.'

'But why is Oliver so convinced that Mr Wymington is bad?' Gillian's face mirrored her confusion. 'There is absolutely nothing evil about him. Surely you just saw that for yourself. What is there not to like about Mr Wymington?'

What was there not to like indeed? Helen thought in the privacy of her room later that evening. She had found Mr Wymington to be all that Gillian claimed him to be; a well-spoken and charming gentleman whose appearance and manners were only to be admired. She did not know him well, of course, but on first meeting, there was nothing to which she could take a dislike.

Unfortunately, Oliver Brandon had made his wishes clear. There was to be absolutely no association between Gillian and Mr Wymington. He had told Mrs Guarding to advise her staff of that fact, so Helen could hardly claim ignorance of his wishes. But what if Oliver's dislike of Mr Wymington had nothing to do with the man personally? What if his feelings of animosity arose from something else altogether? After all, it was not unheard of for fathers or brothers to suffer feelings of jealousy the first time their daughters' or sisters' attentions moved in another direction. Was it possible Oliver was reluctant to lose his stepsister's affections? Because if he was, he could be doing Gillian a tremendous injustice.

Just as your father did you.

Helen closed her eyes and willed the painful thoughts away. No, this was not the time to dwell on that. Their two situations were not the same at all. *Her* father had not wished her to marry beneath her, whereas Mr Brandon did not wish Gillian to marry a fortune-hunter. The reasons for their objections were entirely different.

Unfortunately, when it came right down to it, Helen knew that the end result would be the same. Gillian would not be allowed to follow her heart and marry the man she loved any more than Helen had. The only difference was that Helen was quite sure Gillian would not accept her fate so meekly. Nor that Oliver would escape so lightly!

Oliver tossed back the last of his cognac and stared glumly at his surroundings. He shouldn't have come here tonight. The club was painfully devoid of company. He could usually count on at least one or two of his friends being present but tonight it seemed they had all found better things to do. And he was not in a mood to be alone.

He frowned as he poured himself another drink and crossed one booted ankle over the other. Fact was, he'd been blue-devilled ever since his return from Northamptonshire, and it was all as a result of his encounter with Miss Helen de Coverdale. What was he to make of this young woman who had turned up so unexpectedly in his life again? She was a beauty to be sure. Even now, the memory of her face lingered in his mind like a sweetly haunting melody. But why was he suffering feelings of guilt over what he had said to her? He had only spoken the truth; they'd both known that. And he had only brought the subject up because of Gillian's welfare. So why had Helen glared at him as though *she* had been the injured party?

'Brandon. Good God, man, where the hell've you been?' came an affected drawl behind him. 'Thought perhaps you'd headed for the Americas.'

The husky voice—familiar despite the length of time since he'd heard it—caused Oliver's lip to curl in distaste. He raised his glass in an attempt to disguise his annoyance. 'As you see, I have not.' He glanced up as the man staggered towards the vacant chair across from him. 'Looking a bit foxed this evening, Lord Talbot.'

'Humph, no reason why I shouldn't be.' The heavy man grunted as he sat down. 'Just lost a packet to Clapham! Bloody fool swore he didn't know one card from the other.'

The remark served to restore a little of Oliver's flagging spirits. 'I'm surprised he took you in. Everyone knows Clapham's a master when it comes to cards.'

'Yes, well, I'll be damned if he gulls me like that again. Told him he'd best stay out of my sight.' Talbot raised his hand to summon a waiter. 'So, what brings you to London? Business or pleasure?'

Oliver rested his glass on his knee, but his eyes were sharp on the peer's face. 'A little bit of both.'

'Huh! More pleasure, I'll wager.' Talbot's smile suddenly turned sly. 'Did you know Carter tried to lure your little Nicolette away?'

'Really?' Oliver shrugged, careful not to let his displeasure show. He wasn't concerned that he might lose Nicolette, since it had been some time since he had wished to spend a night in her bed. But he was disappointed that a man who had once called himself a friend had tried to go behind his back in such a way. 'No, I hadn't heard.'

'Didn't think you had. Not that it mattered, because she wouldn't have him.' Talbot reached for the glass the waiter had just brought and downed the contents in one gulp. 'Told him to take himself off. You must keep her well satisfied to make her turn down a nabob like that.'

'We have an understanding,' was all Oliver said.

'Then you're a lucky man. Most wenches would switch beds for nothing more than the promise of a pretty bauble or two.'

'Is that your experience of women?' Oliver enquired mildly.

'For the most part. But there's always more to be had, so I don't trouble myself about it.'

'No, I'm sure you don't.' Oliver steepled his fingers in front of his face. 'Speaking of being lucky, I seem to remember one mistress you must have been sorry to lose.'

Talbot glanced at him in surprise. 'One of mine, you say?'

'Yes. Do you remember the night I caught you and a young lady in the library at Grovesend Hall?'

The peer's expression was blank. 'Grovesend?'

'Yes. Nearly twelve years ago.'

'Good God, man, I barely remember what I was doing twelve *hours* ago, let alone twelve years.'

Oliver smiled faintly. 'I think you would remember this particular night. I walked into the library and found you in an embrace with a young woman by the name of Helen de Coverdale.'

'Helen de…what?'

'Coverdale. I believe she was your governess at the time.'

'A governess.' Talbot's eyes clouded. 'We went through an endless succession of governesses. Why would you expect me to remember one in particular?'

'Because this young lady was exceptional,' Oliver said quietly. 'She had long, black hair, and was, as I recall, exceedingly lovely.'

'Really?' Talbot was silent for a moment. 'Long black hair, you say?'

'Yes.'

'And pretty?'

Oliver filled his glass again. 'Exceptionally.'

It was evident from the look on Talbot's face that his recollection of the past was faulty. So much so, that Oliver began to wonder if he would remember it at all. But then, very slowly, Talbot began to smile. 'Wait a moment. Yes, now that I think about it, I do remember a governess like that. Couldn't tell you what her name was but I remember the long black hair. Fell almost to her waist. And she had the most seductive eyes I'd ever seen.' The peer's smile broadened, but in a way that sent chills down Oliver's spine. 'Yes, damn it, she was beautiful, but she wasn't my mistress.'

Oliver's hand froze halfway to his lips. 'She wasn't?'

'Cold little bitch,' Talbot spat out. 'Wouldn't have anything to do with me. I'd been trying to bed her from the day she walked into the house, but she wouldn't have any part of it. Told me to…well, never mind what she told me to do.'

A flurry of emotions tumbled through Oliver's

mind. 'But you were with her that night. When I walked into the room, you were holding her—'

'Of course I was holding her,' Talbot snapped. 'And I would have done a damn sight more if you hadn't walked in when you had.'

'Then…she wasn't your mistress?'

Talbot shook his head. 'Never so much as kissed her. She left the next morning. Never saw her again. But by God, if ever I did, I wouldn't mind picking up where I left off.' He rose unsteadily from the chair. 'She had the most beautiful… *Ouch!* Damn and blast the bloody table!' he shouted, kicking the offending object aside. He rubbed his hand over the sore spot on his thigh and then limped away, seemingly unaware he'd been halfway through a sentence.

Oliver was more relieved than he cared to admit. What an idiot he'd been. No wonder Miss de Coverdale had been so angry with him. She hadn't been lying to him at all. Obviously, Talbot had come upon her in the library and thought to take advantage of the situation. And Helen, being so much smaller, wouldn't have had a hope of defending herself.

All the way home Oliver thought about the things he'd said to her—and wished he could take every one of them back. Well, there was one thing he knew for a certainty. The moment he concluded his business here, he was going back to Steep Abbot. The sooner he straightened out this mess with Helen, the better.

The only question was, would she be willing to listen to anything he had to say?

In a quiet section of deserted hallway, Helen glanced from the letter in her hands, to Gillian's radiant face, and then back to the letter again. She did not even attempt to hide her feelings of alarm. 'How did Mr Wymington get this to you?'

Gillian was beaming. 'Does it matter?'

'Yes, Gillian, it does. If you are using one of the other girls to pass these notes along, it must stop immediately.'

'But there is nothing in the letter to which anyone could object.' Gillian's happiness shone through her eyes. 'Mr Wymington has simply written to tell me that his uncle's health is improving and that he will soon be returning to Hertfordshire.'

'And that he wishes to see you before he goes.'

'Well, yes, but I am sure it is only because he would like to say goodbye.'

Helen folded up the letter and handed it back to her. 'You must know that I cannot go along with this.'

Gillian's face fell. 'But why not? What does it matter to you if I see him?'

'It matters nothing to me, but it matters a great deal to Mrs Guarding. *And* to the future of this school. What do you think Mr Brandon would say if he were to learn that you had both been seeing *and* receiving correspondence from Mr Wymington, and that I had been privy to it?'

Gillian had the grace to look contrite. 'I imagine he would be a little annoyed, but—'

'He would be *exceedingly* annoyed. So much so that in his anger he might do something to jeopardise the continued operation of this school.'

'Oliver wouldn't do that!'

'Are you so sure?'

For once, Gillian didn't have a ready answer. She merely crossed her arms and walked up and down the length of the room, the jerkiness of her steps evidence of her agitation. 'Then you will not let me see Mr Wymington?'

'I think it best for everyone that you do not.'

Gillian turned and walked the length of the room again. Suddenly, she came to an abrupt halt. 'Wait! I have just had the most marvellous idea. What if I were to meet Mr Wymington—and you were to come with me?'

'*Me!*' Helen gasped.

'Yes. That way you could be sure that nothing untoward was taking place. After all, Mr Wymington could hardly say anything that Oliver would object to if you were standing right there. And since he has suggested that we meet at his uncle's cottage, there will be the presence of another chaperone as well!'

'It is not a question of chaperonage—'

'Oh, please, Miss de Coverdale. I know you think this is wrong, but I do like him so very much. In fact…I love Mr Wymington,' Gillian said, a note of desperation creeping into her voice. 'And I am quite sure he loves me.'

'Has he ever told you that?'

'Not in so many words, but I can tell from the way he behaves when we are together. Oh, please, can you not allow us just this one chance to be together?' Gillian pleaded. 'It would mean so very much to me. And you needn't worry about Mrs Guarding finding out. Since Mr Wymington has said that his uncle's cottage is in the countryside outside Abbot Quincey, there is very little likelihood of anyone seeing us. And I truly have no wish to jeopardise that lady's reputation or the future of the school.'

'I understand that, Gillian, but it is not that simple…'

'If you let me see him just this once, I promise I shan't contact him again,' Gillian implored. 'I shall do as Oliver wishes and apply myself to my studies. I shall be as good as anyone could wish me to be. But please, Miss de Coverdale, please say that you will let me see him. Oliver would not allow me to say goodbye to him before we left Hertfordshire, and I should so very much like to do that now, in person. Is that so terribly wrong?'

Helen breathed out a long, heavy sigh. What a muddle this was turning into. Nothing good could come of allowing a meeting to take place between Gillian and Mr Wymington, she felt sure of it. If Mr Brandon found out, he would be furious. He would certainly take Mrs Guarding to task for her negligence, and then ensure that Helen was made to suffer the consequences. She had to be mad for even *contemplating* such foolishness.

The problem was, though it defied all logic, Helen knew that in some deeply buried part of her heart, she *wanted* Gillian to see her young man one more time. She knew what it was like to be separated from the one you loved. She had not been allowed to see Thomas once her father had learned of her feelings for him, and it had nearly broken her heart. More than that, she remembered how she had felt towards her father after that painful episode. She had come close to hating him for what he had done to her. Did she really wish to be the cause of Gillian resenting Oliver in such a fashion?

Helen took another long, deep breath, and then sent a prayer heavenward that she was not about to do something she would regret for the rest of her life.

'Very well, Gillian. I shall accompany you on a

visit to see Mr Wymington. But I shall remain in the room the entire time, whether his uncle is there or not, and I shall allow the visit to take place *only* on the condition that you do not attempt to see or to correspond with him again. Do I have your agreement?'

'Oh yes, Miss de Coverdale, yes! And thank you so very much! I knew you would understand!'

Helen wasn't sure she understood at all. But there was one other motivating factor she hadn't told Gillian about. One she scarcely liked admitting even to herself.

Retribution. She wanted to strike back at Oliver Brandon for what he had said to her. She wanted to hurt him as much as he had hurt her, and the only way she could do that was through Gillian.

Helen knew it was a dreadful way to feel, and not in the least charitable, but given Oliver's wretchedly unfair opinion of her, she could not help herself. He had not asked her for an explanation as to what had happened with Lord Talbot. He had simply assumed the worst, believing her to be a willing participant in the seduction.

And that was what had angered her the most. It was not the first time Helen had been judged because of her appearance, but that did not mean people had a *right* to believe her prone to certain types of behaviour simply as a result of it. She had never encouraged uninvited attention. Indeed, she went out of her way to avoid it. Unfortunately, some gentlemen seemed to believe that being a governess meant she was ripe for a tumble.

But that was simply not the case. Not even after her father's death, when things had been at their worst, had Helen had any desire to become a man's mistress. She knew it would have afforded her a far more enviable lifestyle than the one she had, but her sense of honour and self-worth were far more important to her than pretty clothes or sparkling baubles.

Yes, she would allow Gillian one last opportunity to see her young man. The child deserved that much. And if Mr Wymington turned out to be the honourable gentleman he seemed, she might even quietly encourage Gillian to keep her hopes up with regards to an eventual match. She would not purposely try to undermine Oliver's authority, but she would remind Gillian that in the fullness of time, she would be in a position to make up her own mind.

Yes, Helen decided with growing certainty. That much she would be willing to do—*if* Mr Wymington turned out to be the kind of man Gillian truly believed he was.

Chapter Seven

Helen did not inform Mrs Guarding of the planned visit to Abbot Quincey for two reasons. The first was because she had no desire to lie to that good lady. The second was because she could not bring herself to feel that what she was doing was entirely wrong. Gillian was not a foolish girl. She was merely a young woman blinded by her feelings. But Helen was not. If it turned out that Mr Wymington was *not* the charming gentleman he pretended to be and that he was only after Gillian's money, Helen felt sure she would be able to see it.

But to do that, she had to spend time in his company. She had to see how he behaved with Gillian. And if she were able to discover any kind of flaws in his personality, she would be in a better position to warn Gillian about them. Surely that was worth any risks that might be involved?

The visit began well enough. Mr Wymington greeted them at the door of the small, well-tended cottage, and then endeavoured to put them at ease by playing the part of the genial host. Gillian, as a result of having been cautioned by Helen beforehand, was somewhat more restrained than usual. She returned his greeting with the proper decorum, and smiled at him in a manner that even a dowager duchess would have approved of.

Helen's only concern was that there was no sign whatsoever of Mr Wymington's uncle.

'Alas, he suffered a bit of a relapse this very afternoon,' Mr Wymington informed them as he led the way into the tiny sitting-room. 'It forced him to retire in something of a foul mood to his bed. He did, however, ask me to pass along his most sincere regrets that he would not be able to make your acquaintance this evening.'

Gillian's disappointment was evident. 'Oh dear. I was so looking forward to meeting him.'

'As he was you, my dear Miss Gresham, but I told him his health must come first. And I live in hope that there will be other opportunities for the two of you to meet.'

'Perhaps you should have Dr Pettifer in to see him,' Helen suggested, anxious to keep the conversation from becoming too personal. 'A relapse can be very serious in a man your uncle's age.'

'I suggested that to him myself, Miss de Coverdale, but he told me that if the good Lord intended to call him home, there was nothing any mortal man could do to stop it.'

'But surely we could pay him a very brief visit?' Gillian persisted. 'Do you not think the sight of two happy, smiling faces would make him feel better?'

Mr Wymington laughed. 'I am sure it would do wonders for his spirits, but I doubt it would do much for his heart. The sight of two such lovely faces stand-

ing by his bed might be more than it could stand. I
know it would put a serious strain on mine.'

Gillian dimpled prettily, obviously finding the remark very much to her liking. Helen did not. She did
not like to believe that Mr Wymington was lying, but
for some reason she was hard pressed to think otherwise. As much as she wanted to believe that the
cottage belonged to his uncle, and that the poor old
gentleman *was* asleep in another room, she was finding it difficult to do so. She couldn't help wondering
if this wasn't all a ruse of some kind; a fabrication
intended to make them believe that it *was* his uncle's
cottage and that Mr Wymington truly had a valid reason for being in the area.

She also wondered if Mr Wymington was really as
pleased to see her as he pretended to be.

In the end, however, Helen was forced to admit that
it was likely only scepticism on her part. Mr
Wymington behaved like a perfect gentleman the entire time. He entertained them with humorous tales of
his adventures in the militia, and served them tea and
biscuits, apologising all the while for the basic fare
and saying that, as a poor bachelor, he was woefully
inexperienced at such feminine arts as entertaining.

Gillian, of course, saw nothing of his faults. She
saw only a handsome gentleman who smiled at her
with uncommon warmth, and whose gaze softened
every time she looked at him. She hung on his every
word and laughed at even the most inconsequential
of his remarks, evidencing no awareness that once
again she was baldly exposing her feelings to him.

Perhaps that was why, as the visit progressed, that
Helen was better able to understand Oliver Brandon's
concerns about his ward's behaviour. There was no

question of Gillian's being infatuated with Mr
Wymington. It was clear that she could—and
would—see absolutely nothing bad about him. And
that was a most precarious position for a young lady
of fortune to be in.

'Well, I think it is time we were on our way, Mr
Wymington,' Helen said abruptly. She placed her cup
and saucer on the small table and stood up. 'Thank
you so much for your hospitality.'

'Yes, it was very good of you to have us,' Gillian
agreed. She also rose, but far more reluctantly than
Helen. 'What a shame the time has gone by so
quickly.'

'It is a shame indeed, Miss Gresham.' Mr
Wymington's voice was warm, his eyes gently caressing as he looked at her. 'But hopefully the months
until you are home again will pass swiftly.'

'They cannot pass swiftly enough for me,' Gillian
cried, forgetting for a moment the warning Helen had
given her.

'Come along, Miss Gresham,' Helen said briskly.
'We must not overstay our welcome.'

'Ah, but you could never outstay your welcome,
Miss de Coverdale,' Mr Wymington said gallantly. 'I
trust you will remember that my door is always open
to you as well as to Miss Gresham.'

The look that accompanied his words was almost
as warm as the one he had given Gillian, and for some
reason, that troubled Helen. She knew there was nothing in his words to which she could take exception,
and yet, once again, she did.

'Thank you, Mr Wymington. But now we really
must be leaving.'

With that, Helen turned to lead the way out of the

cottage. All of a sudden, she was in a desperate hurry to get back to Guarding's.

She shouldn't have come here today. She knew that now. She had made a mistake in allowing Gillian to see this man. Unfortunately, only time would tell how big a mistake it really was, and what would come of it.

After a somewhat prolonged goodbye at the gate, Gillian finally allowed Mr Wymington to hand her up into the carriage. Helen observed the way he held on to her hand, frowning as she saw the manner in which he gently pressed her fingers, and bit her lip when she heard Gillian assure him in the most fervent of tones that she would be counting the days until she was back in Hertfordshire once more.

At last, Mr Wymington turned to smile at her. 'I am so pleased you came along, Miss de Coverdale. And it was very kind of you to arrange this meeting. I am well aware of Mr Brandon's feelings regarding the association between Miss Gresham and myself.'

'It will be the only time, Mr Wymington,' Helen told him quietly. 'Mr Brandon has made his wishes clear with regard to the situation, and while I admit I had my reasons for allowing Miss Gresham to see you today, it will not happen again. I trust you will not endeavour to contact her in the future.'

Mr Wymington inclined his head fractionally. 'Perhaps I can communicate with you directly, Miss de Coverdale. That way you can convey my sentiments to Miss Gresham without anyone being aware of it. For surely *you* are free to receive correspondence from gentlemen?'

Helen glanced at him sharply. 'I am free to receive whatever correspondence I wish, Mr Wymington, but you should know that I am as bound by Mr Brandon's wishes as Miss Gresham is. And I will not violate his trust.'

'Ah, but that is just the thing, Miss de Coverdale,' Mr Wymington said, his voice a silken whisper. 'By bringing Miss Gresham here this afternoon, that is exactly what you have done.'

'Miss de Coverdale, Mr Wymington, what are the two of you whispering about?' Gillian called from the carriage.

Helen sent the girl a worried smile. She was not at all pleased with the way the conversation was going, but she could hardly stand here and continue it now with Gillian only a few feet away and listening to every word they said.

'Mr Wymington, I *beg* you not to pursue this,' Helen said in a low, urgent voice. 'It can have no future. Mr Brandon has made his feelings very clear with regard to you and your relationship with Miss Gresham.'

It seemed to Helen that just for a moment a look of cunning appeared in the man's brilliant blue eyes, replacing the expression of amusement that had been there only moments before. 'I sincerely regret that you have chosen to side with Mr Brandon in this matter, Miss de Coverdale,' he said softly. 'I thought perhaps that by bringing Gillian here this afternoon, you were evidencing sympathy towards our plight. But I see now that such is not the case. However, I am not one to be so easily cast aside.' He reached for her hand and raised it to his lips. 'Perhaps we can arrange to meet, just you and I, to discuss the matter further. Perhaps I can convince you that I am not so shabby a fellow as Mr Brandon would have you believe.'

Then, as he pressed his lips to her hand, he raised his eyes to hers—and Helen felt her insides go cold.

He was looking at her in exactly the same way so many other men had, so many times before.

'Miss de Coverdale, are you coming?' Gillian cried imperiously.

Helen only just managed to conceal her shudder as she withdrew her hand. 'I doubt there will be any need for us to meet again, Mr Wymington. Good day to you, sir.' Then, pausing as she hurried towards the carriage, added, 'I do hope your uncle makes a speedy recovery.'

If Helen had expected him to give himself away, she was again to be disappointed.

'I shall indeed extend the wishes of two such lovely ladies to him,' Mr Wymington said with aplomb. 'Thank you, Miss de Coverdale. *Arrivederci ad un altro giorno.*'

Helen's foot faltered on the step. The expression, spoken in near-perfect Italian, was not one to signify a farewell. It simply meant goodbye—until another day.

Gillian waited all of twenty seconds before commencing the inquisition.

'There, *now* what do you think of my dear Mr Wymington?' she demanded, clearly very pleased with herself and with the visit. 'Is he not a perfect gentleman? Is he not as wonderful as I have been telling you?'

'He is a handsome gentleman with very nice manners,' Helen forced herself to say, 'but beyond that, I do not believe I am in a position to offer any kind of informed opinion about him. I still know very little of his character.'

'But how can you say that? Did you not hear him evidence concern towards his uncle? Did you not find his stories amusing, and his speech and company all that could be admired?'

Helen turned away to hide her sigh. It was painful having to listen to Gillian go on about the man. The excitement and hopefulness in her voice was evidence of her infatuation, and it was obvious that she wanted Helen to share that enthusiasm.

Helen could understand that. Had she been Gillian's age, and at her stage in life, she would probably have felt the same way. But she wasn't Gillian's age and she certainly wasn't in her situation. At one-and-thirty, Helen had far more experience of life than Gillian ever would. She knew what motivated men like Sidney Wymington, and she was deeply troubled by their meeting this afternoon. Certain aspects of his character worried her, as did the manner in which they had parted. If what Helen was beginning to suspect was true, Gillian was destined to fall very hard when she learned the truth about him.

But even more frightening than that, was whether or not she would learn the truth before it was too late!

Helen was tidying her room after the last class of the day when she heard the sound of a knock on the door. She turned around—and drew a startled breath. 'Mr Brandon!'

'Good afternoon, Miss de Coverdale. I hope I haven't come at a bad time?' he said hesitantly.

Helen glanced at him in surprise. His voice lacked the hard edge it had held before, and there was something almost apologetic in his tone. Nevertheless, she kept her voice cool as she leaned against the edge of her desk, suddenly finding herself in need of its support. 'A bad time for what?'

'To speak with you?'

'I thought we had said all that needed to be said.'

Oliver took two steps into the room. 'On the contrary, there is a great deal more I would say to you. If you will give me the chance.'

Helen's first impulse was to say no. After all, what more could he possibly wish to say? What other insults had he to fling at her? Then, she glanced into his eyes and saw something that gave her pause. 'What is this about, Mr Brandon?'

'Something which is very important to both of us. But especially to you.'

Something important to her? Helen sighed. 'Very well. I have a few minutes before tea. What have you to say to me that is so terribly important?'

'I wonder...' Oliver glanced around the room. 'Is there somewhere we might go that would be more conducive to conversation?'

For the first time, Helen allowed herself a smile. 'I have always found my classroom to be most conducive to conversation, Mr Brandon. It is one of the functions it serves.'

To her surprise, Oliver smiled too. 'Yes, I am sure it is. But I think it is still quite pleasant outside. Perhaps you would care to join me for a stroll about the gardens?'

Deciding that a breath of fresh air might not be such a bad idea, Helen picked up her shawl and draped it over her shoulders. She led the way to the backstairs and then out into the late afternoon sunshine. Soon, they were walking together down the length of the gravelled drive. The large trees provided cover from both the road and the school and would, with any luck, prevent her from being treated to a barrage of questions in class tomorrow morning about the gentleman she had been seen strolling with this afternoon.

'Very well, Mr Brandon, we are outside in surroundings which are hopefully more conducive to adult conversation,' Helen said, trying to keep the sarcasm from her voice. 'What is it you wish to say to me?'

'To tell you the truth, Miss de Coverdale, I hardly know where to begin,' Oliver admitted slowly. 'I fear the errors I have made are grievous indeed. But I suppose I should commence by extending my most humble apologies for the mistake I made so many years ago, and for the tremendous embarrassment I have caused you as a result.'

It was not at all what Helen had been expecting to hear. An apology? From Oliver Brandon?

Too shocked to do more than stare at him, Helen waited for him to continue.

'By chance I met someone in London a few nights ago,' Oliver continued. 'Someone with whom we are both acquainted, but whom neither of us has seen in a very long time.'

The remark brought a frown to Helen's face. 'I cannot imagine who you are talking about, sir. There are few people I know in London any more.'

'Nevertheless, this is someone with whom you are acquainted. And not happily, I regret to say.' When Helen continued to look blank, Oliver said softly, 'Lord Talbot.'

The name caused Helen to stumble awkwardly. *Lord Talbot!*

Immediately, Oliver reached for her, the warmth of his hand closing firmly around her arm. 'Are you all right?'

'Yes, I'm…fine. That was clumsy of me. I wasn't watching where I was going.' Helen pretended to concentrate on the ground ahead of her, but all she could see was Lord Talbot's face. It loomed like a dark spectre in her mind, bringing back all of the unpleasant memories of the past. She was also aware of Oliver's hand still resting on her arm, and of the comforting warmth it offered. 'Please…go on.'

'I chanced to encounter Talbot at my club.' Oliver withdrew his hand as they walked on. 'And as is so often the case, he had been drinking. Apparently, he had just lost a large sum of money to a man most gamblers know to avoid.'

'Mr Brandon, I have no wish to hear about Lord Talbot's losses or about his drunkenness,' Helen interrupted. 'In fact, I have no wish to hear *anything* about him.'

'Not even a confession he made to me whilst in his cups?'

'No, because I cannot imagine what kind of confession he might make to you that would be of any interest to me.'

'What about one which pertained to that infamous night in the library?'

Helen stared at him in surprise. Then, warily, she nodded. 'Go on.'

'Lord Talbot admitted to me that he had forced himself upon you that night,' Oliver said. 'He told me it had been his intention to seduce you from the mo-

ment you first walked into his house. He also told me
that you refused to have anything to do with him.'

Helen listened to his words, too surprised by what
he was saying to offer any kind of comment. She
knew she should have been delighted at hearing
Oliver Brandon—the only other person who had been
a witness to her humiliation—say that she was not to
blame for what had happened. She should have been
happy and relieved that after all this time, she had
finally been vindicated.

And yet, she wasn't ecstatic or happy or even particularly relieved. It was almost as though he was
talking about someone else. Someone she didn't know
any more. All she felt was a strange kind of numbness
around her heart. Because when it came right down
to it, what had she really gained from Lord Talbot's
admission?

Yes, Oliver Brandon now knew that she hadn't
been to blame for any part of the seduction he'd witnessed that night. But that did not change the fact that
he'd had to hear it from Lord Talbot himself before
he'd given it any credence. He hadn't rushed to ask
her about the truth of the matter. In fact when she
had tried to tell him, he had put his own interpreta-
tions on it and, once again, made her feel culpable.

Furthermore, Helen knew that the *only* reason the
peer had made *any* admission of guilt was because
he'd been in his cups. Had he been sober, he would
never have embarrassed himself by admitting that a
lowly governess had spurned his advances.

'Thank you for telling me, Mr Brandon. It is…
good to know that your fears have finally been laid
to rest.' Helen managed a fleeting smile. 'Hopefully,
you will no longer worry about the time Gillian

and I spend together, or about any topics we might choose to discuss. And now, I think I should return to the school.'

'But…is that all you have to say to me?' Oliver reached for her arm and turned her around to face him. 'After the shoddy way I treated you, have you no words of reprisal? No harsh expressions of condemnation? I thought you would have been pleased with the news.'

Helen sighed. 'I see nothing to be pleased at in being told something I already knew, sir. It was you who jumped to the conclusion that I was in the library with Lord Talbot of my own choice. You put your own interpretation on what you saw there and you weren't inclined to believe me when I tried to tell you differently, so I fail to understand why I should feel happy now that you have finally learned the truth from someone else.'

Oliver appeared taken aback by her response. 'I simply thought you might have enjoyed being given the opportunity of telling me I was wrong.'

Helen tried to rally a smile, but this time, even that simple gesture eluded her. 'It really doesn't matter what you think any more. I have tried to put the past behind me and move on with my life. Your coming here and reminding me of what happened twelve years ago forced me to take an unpleasant step backwards, but that is all. I was foolish to let your bad opinion weigh upon my mind, and I would be even more foolish to allow myself comfort now that you have changed it. A great man once said that truth is always the strongest argument. I have always believed that to be the case. Sometimes, it is just a matter of waiting for others to recognise it. And now, I would bid you a good afternoon, Mr Brandon. And… goodbye.'

Chapter Eight

Helen was quite sure that her conversation with Oliver would be the last one she would ever have with him. He had offered his explanation and his apology, and as far as she was concerned, the matter was closed. She saw no reason for their paths to cross again, except, perhaps, as it concerned Gillian. To her surprise, however, Oliver seemed reluctant to let it go. It was almost as though he felt obliged to make up for the error in judgement he had made all those years ago, and for the embarrassment he had caused her as a result. So when Gillian told her that he was planning an outing to Castle Ashby, and that she was to be included, Helen had naturally felt compelled to object.

'But there is no reason for Mr Brandon to include me on such an outing. Our acquaintance is not of the kind that would warrant my being invited to participate in a family excursion of this kind.'

'But did you not say you would enjoy visiting the castle if you ever had an opportunity to do so?' Gillian retorted.

'Of course, but that does not mean I thought to do

so with you and Mr Brandon.' Helen's brow furrowed as she walked around the empty classroom collecting slates. 'I hope *you* did not suggest to your guardian that I come along.'

'Well, I suppose I *might* have mentioned your passion for the Italian Renaissance once or twice,' the girl admitted. 'And I understand that Castle Ashby has a particularly fine collection of paintings from the period, as well as some splendid tapestries.'

'Be that as it may, it was still no reason to ask Mr Brandon to include me in your visit. If he has arranged an outing, it is because he wishes to spend time with *you*.'

'But he told me I might bring along whomever I wished. And when I thought about everything Castle Ashby had to offer from an educational point of view, I immediately thought of you.'

Helen pressed her lips together. She was beginning to understand why Mr Brandon felt it necessary to warn people about his ward. Gillian was very good at getting her own way, but in such a manner that one seldom felt as though one was being manipulated. Such was the case here, in that an innocent family outing had suddenly become an opportunity for an *educational* experience.

'Oh, do say you will come with us, Miss de Coverdale,' Gillian urged as the silence dragged on. 'It would make the outing far more enjoyable for me. And I am sure Oliver would be grateful for your company.'

'Grateful?'

'Yes. He often complains that my constant chattering about inconsequential matters bores him excessively.'

Helen found the notion of Mr Brandon's being grateful for having her along for *any* reason hard to accept. Why would he, when she was little more than a stranger to him?

'Besides, if it makes you feel any better, I have also asked Elizabeth Brookwell to join us,' Gillian said. 'Her mother is a good friend of Sophie's, so he can have no concerns about the connection.'

'Yes, but will he not mind the intrusion of yet another person? I cannot help but feel that his desire to spend time with you has suddenly blossomed into a full-blown party.'

'Oliver won't mind.' Gillian gave her a confident smile. 'He can be very accommodating when he wishes to be.'

'I am surprised to hear you in such charity with him,' Helen remarked. 'I thought you were still angry at him for sending you here.'

'Oh, I always *get* angry with Oliver, but I seldom stay angry with him. I am not *happy* with him for taking me away from Mr Wymington, of course, but I did promise I would not mention that subject again, so I shall not. But I can assure you that Oliver will be pleased to hear I have invited you and Elizabeth along. Besides, four is a much nicer number than three for an outing, don't you think?'

Helen made no reply, for in truth, she could not think of one. She wasn't even sure that anything she might say *would* make a difference. Gillian's mind was made up and she was beginning to learn that once it was, there was very little chance of it being changed.

But what about Oliver Brandon? How would he feel about having her come along when only a few

days ago she had told him, in no uncertain terms,
exactly what she thought of him and of his apology!

On the appointed day, Oliver arrived at the
Guarding Academy at promptly half-past twelve.
And, as Gillian had predicted, he did not seem in the
least concerned at the prospect of escorting three
ladies to Castle Ashby, rather than one. In fact, he
seemed decidedly pleased at the unexpected mix of
company awaiting him. He settled the two giggling
girls in the carriage first, and then turned to offer his
hand to Helen.

'I am delighted you agreed to join us, Miss de
Coverdale. Gillian told me she had invited you but I
was not sure you would come.'

A blush danced across Helen's cheeks. 'Your ward
can be very persuasive when she wishes to be, Mr
Brandon. She all but told me that because the visit
was to be of an educational nature it would be remiss
of me, as her teacher, not to come along.
Unfortunately, she also appealed to my love of art
and that made it very difficult for me to refuse.'

Oliver's eyes crinkled with amusement. 'Then I am
grateful for Gillian's *persuasiveness*, as you have so
nicely phrased it. There have been times in the past
when I have been tempted to call it otherwise, but
since it has convinced you to make up one of our
party, I shall not condemn her for it. And now, let us
be off. A most pleasurable day awaits.'

Castle Ashby was a sprawling Elizabethan house
set in the countryside six miles east of Northampton.
It had been built in the early sixteen hundreds and
contained a wealth of paintings from the Italian

Renaissance period, along with fine examples of the
seventeenth-century Dutch school. Oliver had already
determined that the Marquis and Marchioness of
Northampton were not at home, and so had applied
to the housekeeper to show them around.

The girls exclaimed at length over the elegant fur-
nishings and priceless hangings inside many of the
rooms, and while they were initially awed by the
stateliness and grandeur of the house, they both
agreed they would be most happy to be mistress of
such a fine establishment. Helen would have preferred
them to stay close, but they were more inclined to
walk ahead, talking in excited whispers, and leaving
her frequently in the company of Mr Brandon alone.

Helen was very conscious of his eyes on her as
they stopped in the dining-room to admire the beautiful dishes and exquisite appointments. She felt very
plain indeed against the opulence all around her, and
suddenly wished she'd had something more fashion-
able to wear than the plain muslin dress under a man-
tle of twilled sarcenet. But she knew it would have
been foolish to spend her hard-earned wages on such
unnecessary extravagances. A stylish pelisse like the
one Gillian was wearing, or even the shorter one
Elizabeth sported, would have cost far more than her
meagre income allowed.

Fortunately, Mr Brandon did not seem displeased
with her appearance. In fact, Helen was quite sure she
saw a flicker of admiration in his eyes, and she took
comfort in the knowledge that she was not an embarrassment to him. *Why* she should worry about what
Oliver Brandon thought of her, she would not even
allow herself to consider.

'Have you visited Castle Ashby before, Miss de

Coverdale?' Oliver enquired as they slowly walked the length of the picture gallery.

Helen shook her head. 'I have not had the pleasure, sir. I've often thought it would be a splendid house to see, but there is seldom a carriage available to bring us this distance, and I would not undertake a journey like this on my own.'

'Then I hope you see all you wish to today so that you can remember it long after you have returned to Guarding's.'

Helen risked a quick glance at him as he stopped to admire a particularly fine painting of the current Marquis's father. She wished she could bring herself to feel more at ease in his company, but something about him made her feel gauche and tongue-tied. Which was silly, given that he had done nothing but try to make her feel at ease ever since they had left the school.

'It was very good of you to allow me to come today, Mr Brandon,' Helen said, feeling it was the least she could do. 'I cannot help but feel that I have intruded on a family outing.'

'On the contrary, you have spared me the tedium of having to listen to the unending chatter of two excitable young girls.' A wry but indulgent glint appeared in Oliver's eyes. 'You offer far more interesting and intelligent comments about the paintings and their artists than I would have heard otherwise, Miss de Coverdale, and I confess myself impressed by the depth of your knowledge.'

His candid answer brought a smile to Helen's lips. 'I would be a poor teacher indeed if I did not know more about my subject than my pupils. But I own, it is a pleasure to talk to someone who is truly *interested* in the subject, rather than to a group of girls who learn it because they know they must.'

'I can understand your feeling that way. When I was at school, there were many subjects I learned because I had to rather than because I wished to. I suppose it is the nature of education.' Oliver hesitated, and then gruffly cleared his throat. 'I am also pleased you agreed to come today, because I was not sure you would *wish* to be in my company again, given the nature of our last conversation.'

Helen purposely fixed her gaze on the painting in front of her. So he too had suffered doubts as a result of that meeting. She was glad, and even a little relieved. Mayhaps Oliver Brandon was not as narrowminded as she had come to believe.

'I do not recall there being anything in our speech to make you feel that way,' she replied. 'A misunderstanding was laid to rest and the air cleared between us, but that is all, I think. We did not part in anger.'

'No, but I know I offended you, and I regret that very much,' Oliver said quietly. 'You were right to express your disappointment in my behaviour, for I can assure you I felt it most keenly myself.'

Helen raised her eyes to his and was momentarily shaken by the expression she saw within them. 'I…thank you for telling me, sir, but as I said before, what happened in the past is over and done with. Perhaps it would be best for both of us if that is where we left it.'

His gaze travelled over her face, touching briefly on her mouth, and then searching her eyes. 'You are a most admirable woman, Miss de Coverdale. I was wrong to think otherwise.'

Having no answer to give him, Helen merely inclined her head, and the two walked on in silence.

'Gillian seems to be settling well into her new environment,' Oliver commented when they had walked on some way.

Relieved that the conversation had taken a more neutral turn, Helen smiled. 'Yes, I believe her initial feelings of resistance have been overcome. The staff are all delighted with her progress and she is very popular with the girls, especially the younger ones.'

'I am glad to hear it.' Oliver clasped his hands behind his back and moved towards the next painting. 'In truth, I did not know if sending her to Mrs Guarding's Academy was the right thing to do. My sister, Sophie, suggested it. She spoke very highly of the school's reputation and of Mrs Guarding herself and it was she who convinced me of the wisdom of sending Gillian there.'

'To finish her education?' Helen couldn't resist asking.

Oliver slanted her a rueful glance. 'That, and to distance her from Mr Wymington.'

Helen bit her lip and looked away. Her feelings of guilt at having broken the rules and allowed a meeting to take place between Gillian and Mr Wymington were growing by the day, but she was still not convinced that Oliver Brandon's reasons for wishing to keep the two apart were entirely justified.

'Gillian seems to think you are being unfair in not allowing her to see Mr Wymington,' Helen said, deciding this might be a good time to find out. 'Is he really so unsuitable?'

'If you were to meet him you would not think so.' Oliver bent forward to study the detail on the painting in front of him. 'From outward appearances, he is all that is charming.'

'Then why do you object to him?'

'Because I do not trust him. I do not believe for a moment that his intentions towards my ward are honourable.'

'You do not believe that he is in love with her?'

Oliver turned towards her and his burning eyes held her still. 'I believe it is her fortune to which he is most keenly attracted, Miss de Coverdale. I think he merely gives the impression of caring for Gillian in order to disguise his true intent.'

'That is a strong accusation to make without proof.'

Oliver shrugged. 'Perhaps, but how would you suggest I go about obtaining such proof? If I were to ask him the nature of his feelings, he would hardly be so foolish as to tell me something I did not wish to hear.'

'Do you not think you would be able to tell the difference between feigned affections and those which are genuine? Surely if Mr Wymington was only pretending to love Gillian, something in his voice or his manners would give him away.'

Oliver sighed. 'Even if that were the case, what good would it do me? Gillian is the one who must be convinced of his unsuitability, not I.'

'Mr Brandon, have you given any consideration to the possibility that what you are looking for simply isn't there?'

'I beg your pardon?'

Helen knew she was delving into matters that were, by all rights, none of her business, but given what was at stake, she felt she had the right to ask. She'd already begun to suspect that Oliver was correct about Mr Wymington's character, but she needed to know if his reservations stemmed from feelings of genuine mistrust, or from something more personal.

'Perhaps you can find nothing to object to in Mr Wymington's manner because there is nothing to object to.'

Oliver studied her in enigmatic silence for a moment. Then he said, 'Women put much stock in intuition, do they not, Miss de Coverdale?'

'Yes, I suppose we do.'

'Well, it may surprise you to hear it, but so do I. Mr Wymington has done absolutely nothing for which I can fault him,' he told her candidly. 'There are no marks against his service record, nor any man willing to speak out against him. And yet, something here,' Oliver pointed to the area just below his heart, 'tells me he is not to be trusted. I believe the words he speaks are not the sentiments of his heart, and I am afraid that if I allow Gillian to marry him, I would be making a most grievous mistake.' Oliver's mouth curved in a sad, almost wistful smile. 'Ours is not a perfect world, Miss de Coverdale. I doubt either of us is so foolish as to believe that the majority of marriages are made for love. And yet, in Gillian's case, I find myself hoping that the man who marries her will do so *because* he loves her, rather than because he has any less noble reasons at heart.'

A smile tugged reluctantly at Helen's mouth. 'Your confession is safe with me, Mr Brandon, but I do hope you are not wrong about Mr Wymington. Sometimes the biggest mistakes are made by those who have the best intentions of others at heart.'

His gaze held hers momentarily. 'You sound like you speak from experience. Might I hazard a guess that something similar has happened in your life?'

'Oliver?' Gillian suddenly called from the bottom of the stairs, 'when are you and Miss de Coverdale coming down? Elizabeth and I are anxious to see the gardens.'

'We are coming now,' Oliver replied calmly. 'Go ahead and we shall meet you there.'

'Very well. But do not be long! There is so much to see, we would not wish to leave you behind.'

Helen carefully bit back a smile. At times it was hard to tell who had brought whom on the excursion today. In truth, however, she was not ungrateful for Gillian's interruption. Oliver's question had caught her off guard and she hadn't known what to say. She could no more imagine telling him about her own unhappy love affair than she could believe he would be interested in hearing about it. And yet, just for a moment, something in his eyes had reached out to her; almost making her want to talk about some of the secrets she had locked away so deeply in her heart.

They made their way back outside, and once there, Helen stopped to admire the beautiful countryside in front of her. 'How lovely it all is,' she whispered. 'I do not think I could ever grow tired of looking at such beauty.'

'The view is very fine to be sure,' Oliver agreed, 'though I feel I am the more fortunate one. From where I stand I have the benefit of two very different but equally lovely views.'

Helen was not of an age to pretend an ignorance of what he was saying, yet the softness of his voice and the genuine warmth with which he offered his compliment caused her to blush like a schoolgirl. 'You are too kind, Mr Brandon.'

'Kindness has very little to do with it, Miss de Coverdale. ' He indicated a bench where they might sit down. 'You are a remarkably beautiful woman, and I am sure I am not the first to tell you that. But come, enough of flattery. You said that something similar had happened in your life. Would you not be willing to tell me about it?'

Once again, Oliver's seemingly genuine desire to learn about her past put Helen in a definite quandary. What possible good could come of revealing intimate details of her life to him? There was certainly no romantic interest between them. It was not as though he needed to know things about her that might help determine her suitability to becoming his wife. So what interest could he possibly have in hearing about what had happened in her past?

Helen mulled that over for a while. As she did, however, she began to wonder whether divulging something about her own past might not help Gillian now. Perhaps by disclosing details of her own thwarted love, she might be better able to make him understand what she was trying to say. Was that not worth the embarrassment such a disclosure would bring about?

'It seems a long time ago now,' Helen began reluctantly. 'And indeed, it is in the measure of years. But I still remember how…difficult it was at the time.' She took a deep breath and then raised her eyes to his. 'When I was little more than Gillian's age, my father prevented me from…marrying the man I loved.'

Oliver's gaze remained steady on her face, but his eyes were suddenly filled with questions. 'I assume he had a good reason for doing so?'

'He believed he did. My father informed me that…the gentleman was beneath me in every way, and that I was foolish to have allowed my feelings to become engaged. He told me that as his daughter, I could do better than to marry a poor clergyman.'

'I see.' Oliver eyes were dark, the expression in them unreadable. 'And were you truly in love with your poor clergyman, Miss de Coverdale?'

There was no mockery in his voice, not even a hint of reprisal. Only a gentle note of concern that told her he was not unsympathetic to her plight. Nevertheless, Helen turned away, strangely uncomfortable at talking to Oliver about her involvement with another man. 'Yes, I loved him,' she admitted. 'Thomas was extremely dedicated to his calling, and to the people in his care. He had great hopes for the parish and for the work he wanted to do there.' Her smile grew unknowingly wistful. 'I believe his passion for his work and for other people was part of what I loved about him.'

'And do you love him still?'

Helen raised startled eyes to his. 'It was a very long time ago.'

'Perhaps, but I have heard that first loves are often the hardest to forget.'

He had heard. So Gillian was right. Oliver Brandon hadn't been in love, for if he had, he would surely have remembered the pains and the pleasures of his very first *affaire de coeur*.

'I suppose they are, but time changes many things.' Suddenly restless, Helen got to her feet. 'In the years that followed, my life went through many changes, none of which were particularly pleasant. My mother died, and after her death my father just seemed to give up. He lost all interest in life. He stopped going to work, and eventually began to drink. I suppose he did so to forget the pain, but it made life very difficult for those close to him. He died less than a year later. By that time, we had amassed such a staggering debt that it became necessary to sell the house just to cover the tradesmen's bills and the cost of the servants' wages.'

'Is that when you were forced to seek employment?'

Helen nodded, but did not look at him. 'I had no choice. I had no relatives in England with whom I could stay, and I had lost touch with my mother's family in Italy, so there was nothing I could do but look for a paying position.'

'What about your clergyman? What did he do when he learned of your troubles?'

Helen fixed her gaze on a distant field. 'He never did. Thomas married within six months of our parting. He moved to Derbyshire soon after and was given the living of a fine church there.'

'That must have come as a great disappointment to you.'

'Young men in the church are often ambitious, Mr Brandon. Thomas knew the Dean wished him to take a wife, and since it was not going to be me, he chose…someone else.'

'Pity he did not wait a little longer,' Oliver commented wryly. 'Had he done so, he would have been able to have both the woman he loved *and* the life he'd chosen for himself.'

Helen said nothing. There didn't seem to be any point in admitting that she had often wondered about the same thing herself. 'Sometimes it is best that we not know what is around the next corner. If we did, we might be tempted to spend our entire lives waiting for tomorrow to arrive.'

Oliver studied her face, and then reached out to gently brush his fingers against her cheek. 'Sometimes tomorrow is worth waiting for, Miss de Coverdale. We just have to be wise enough to realise it at the time.'

The touch of his hand and the softness in his voice were nearly Helen's undoing. She could not risk exposing any more of her vulnerabilities to him. It was too easy to get lost in the tenderness of his gaze. Too easy to read meanings into words that weren't there.

'Oliver, Miss de Coverdale, come quickly!' Gillian cried from further down the garden. 'We have found the most delightful gazebo hidden in the trees. Oh, do come and look!'

The intrusion of the high-pitched voice into her conversation with Oliver came as a relief to Helen. It shattered the mood of intimacy that had begun to form between them, and brought her abruptly back to earth. 'I think we had best rejoin the girls, Mr Brandon. No doubt they will be wondering at our constantly lagging behind.'

'I shouldn't worry about it,' Oliver said, nevertheless getting to his feet. 'They will put it down to our age, as young people are inclined to do.'

Helen smiled and would have walked on had she not felt the gentle pressure of his hand on her arm. 'Thank you for telling me about your young man, Miss de Coverdale. I know it was not an easy admission. But given the situation between Gillian and Mr Wymington, I can understand why you felt I needed to know.'

Helen looked down at his hand, aware of the warmth emanating from it, and gave him a regretful smile. 'It was not only because of Gillian's feelings for Mr Wymington I told you this, Mr Brandon, but because of her feelings for *you*.'

'I'm not sure I understand.'

Helen took a deep breath. 'After my father forbade me to see Thomas, my feelings towards him began to change. I could not understand why he would not allow me to see the man I loved, nor condone a relationship neither my mother nor I saw anything wrong with. But my father would not change his mind, and I resented him for that. Nor did I ever fully forgive him.'

'Is that what you see happening between Gillian and myself?'

'I cannot speak for your ward, sir, but the situations are not so very different. Gillian doesn't understand why you do not wish her to see Mr Wymington, any more than I understood why my father refused to allow me to see Thomas. But I fear that if you forbid the association outright, there is a good chance she will come to feel the same kind of resentment towards you that I felt towards my father. And I would truly hate to see that happen. I know how much Gillian loves and respects you, but sometimes, in the foolishness of youth and the idealistic fantasies of love, young women lose sight of that.'

Oliver was silent for a few minutes. Then, he nodded. 'Your compassion does you credit, Miss de Coverdale, as does your loyalty to my ward. But I'm afraid it is a risk I shall have to take. Gillian might only be a stepsister to me, but I love her as dearly as I do my own sister, and because of her impulsive nature, I worry about her twice as much. I would not wish to see her marry ill and find out too late that she has been deceived. I would never forgive myself if that happened. For as you've said yourself, a mistake once made, no matter how innocently, stays with us for a very long time. Isn't that right, my dear Miss de Coverdale?'

Chapter Nine

Helen thought about what Oliver had said for a long time after she returned to the school: '*…a mistake once made, no matter how innocently, stays with us for a very long time…*'

Had he been referring to the mistake he'd made with her twelve years ago? Helen thought it likely, given the note of regret she had heard in his voice. She also remembered what he'd said about Mr Wymington, and the more she thought about it, the more she realised that he was right. Mr Wymington was not as harmless as he seemed; a conclusion confirmed a few days later when a small parcel arrived from the gentleman. The package was addressed to Helen but inside was a sealed enclosure for Gillian.

The remarks Mr Wymington made in his note to Helen were both pleasant and innocuous, expressing again his delight at having met her and at having seen them both in Abbot Quincey. But they were also followed by a request that she forward the enclosed letter to Miss Gresham at her earliest convenience.

Helen did not pass the note along, of course, nor had she any intention of doing so. But when a second letter arrived a few days later, accompanied by a note which suggested in more forceful terms that she forward the letter, Helen knew she had to do something. It seemed she had not mistaken the look in Mr Wymington's eyes. He was just as determined as Gillian when it came to getting what he wanted—and what he wanted was Gillian.

Helen thought back to some of the remarks he had made just before she and Gillian had taken their leave of him, and in particular, to the remark he had made about Helen having compromised herself by allowing Gillian and Mr Wymington to meet. Had he intended the remark as a threat? Helen hadn't thought much about it at the time, but now she realised it was a very good possibility. Was it also his plan to tell Oliver what she had done if she did not allow him to see Gillian or to allow her to receive correspondence from him?

Helen couldn't be sure, but she knew it was imperative that she find out. She had inadvertently put herself in an exceedingly awkward position and the only way she could see her way clear to getting out of it was by being truthful to all. There would be time enough to worry about the consequences later.

So saying, she sat down at her desk and wrote another letter to Mr Wymington, asking him to do her the favour of meeting with her. She told him they had a most urgent matter to discuss, and suggested they meet in Abbot Giles, the village the farthest removed from the school. She then addressed the letter to his uncle's cottage in Abbot Quincey and gave it to one of the kitchen lads to post.

Not that it would matter if anyone did see her, Helen reflected as she threw her shawl about her

shoulders and went out for a walk. No one apart from
Gillian and herself knew what Mr Wymington looked
like, so if anyone did see them together, she could
simply say she had run into an old friend. But she
knew she couldn't afford to wait any longer. She had
to speak to Mr Wymington and find out exactly what
his intentions towards Gillian were. Because the
sooner she did, the sooner she could tell Oliver
Brandon that he was wrong—or right—in his assumptions about the man.

Not surprisingly, at the thought of Oliver Brandon,
Helen experienced again the strange fluttery sensation
in the pit of her stomach. She was astonished at how
much her feelings towards him had changed. She was
no longer angry or even resentful about what he *believed* had taken place with Lord Talbot. Indeed, she
had been touched by Oliver's apology and by his concern that she understand the reasons behind it. More
than that, during their outing to Castle Ashby, she had
been given a glimpse into another side of the man.
She had experienced first-hand his concern for his
ward, and she had listened to him express his own
doubts as to the wisdom of what he was doing for her
now.

On a more personal note, Helen had found herself
opening up to him and telling him personal things
about her own life and even about her feelings for
Thomas. And he had been a marvellous listener. At
no time had she felt that she was boring him, or that
he was listening to her out of a sense of obligation.
His interest in her past had been genuine, as had the
look of concern in his eyes when she had revealed
her feelings of resentment towards her father.

Yes, something had definitely happened between

them at Castle Ashby. Unfortunately, Helen suspected it wasn't anything good. At least, not for her. She had begun to care about a man who had never known what it was like to be in love. She had given her heart to someone who would not only not want it, but who would likely have no idea what to do with it once he discovered it was in his possession.

Oliver spent the days following his outing to Castle Ashby in something of a brown study. Because it wasn't the castle or his ward that lingered on his mind, but Helen de Coverdale. Certainly, he couldn't deny that his opinion of her had changed over the last few weeks. Whereas for the past eleven years he had believed her to be a beautiful, sensual woman willing to use her appearance and her feminine wiles to make her way in the world, he now realised how wrong he had been. Helen had been nothing more than a victim of circumstances; a woman trapped by her own beauty in a situation totally beyond her control. What he had seen of her that night in the library had not been a tempting seductress trying to coax money or jewels from her lover, but an innocent young woman fighting for her virtue.

Why the hell hadn't he seen it at the time? Oliver demanded of himself. Had he been so blind to the truth that he hadn't been able to see the look of unbridled lust on Talbot's face and the unmistakable look of fear on hers? Because it was all he *could* see now that he thought back to that night. Unfortunately, it had taken an admission from Lord Talbot himself to force Oliver to look back and see beyond his own ignorance.

It was a wonder Helen was even speaking to him!

Still, perhaps it was a good thing it had taken such a jolt to make him see the truth, Oliver reflected. Because her graciousness in accepting his apology was just another indication of the kind of woman she really was. He saw the patience she exhibited towards her pupils, and the gentleness with which she talked to the little girls. And he had seen more than once her willingness to laugh. Would he ever forget the look in Helen's eyes when she had turned to find one of her girls spattered in paint? There had certainly been no anger in her expression. Indeed, she had been forced to bite her lip to keep from laughing. She was a warm and caring woman who gave more to others than she asked for herself. And in doing so, she commanded affection from her girls, respect from her peers, and the unwavering loyalty of the woman who employed her.

As to hearing that Helen had been in love with another man, Oliver hadn't wanted to admit, even to himself, his feelings upon learning that. Certainly there was no reason for him to have had *any* kind of feelings in the matter. Nor had he the heart to tell her that had he been in her father's place, he would probably have done the same thing. He knew better than most the social implications of such a marriage. But when Helen's life had been turned upside down by her father's death, and she had been forced to make her own way in the world, she had done so with courage and dignity. Not, as he'd first believed, through the use of artifice and temptation.

Yes, there was much to admire in Helen de Coverdale, Oliver acknowledged, and he cursed himself for the ridiculous concerns he'd entertained. Imagine believing that she would be a bad influence on his ward. In point of fact, Gillian would do well to study the example set by such a woman. And that was something else Oliver was pleased about. Gillian was in a much better frame of mind than she had been when he'd left her at the school a few weeks ago. She seemed to have made a place for herself there, and he was delighted with her association with Elizabeth Brookwell, whom he knew to be a nicely mannered young lady from a good family.

More than that, however, Oliver was relieved that Gillian had not made a single mention of Mr Wymington. She had not acted the part of a lovelorn waif nor professed herself wretched with despair. Instead, she had laughed and acted like a young woman who hadn't a care in the world.

Yes, Sophie had been right in her suggestion that he send Gillian to Steep Abbot. Oliver had no doubt that by the time she returned to Hertfordshire at the end of the year she would be over her infatuation with Mr Wymington and eager to travel to London for the Season. Hopefully, she would meet a man more suitable to her station and they would marry and settle down, leaving Oliver free to get on with his own life.

And then suddenly, it hit him. What did he *want* to do with the rest of his life? What was he to do once Gillian married and moved away? How would he keep himself occupied in the empty halls of Shefferton Hall?

And why did an image of Helen de Coverdale keep popping up in his mind?

Abbot Giles lay due west of the Guarding Academy. It was a small village, boasting a church and a vicarage, and it could be reached by walking through the grounds of the Abbey, a building that until a few months ago had been the home of the contemptible Marquis of Sywell.

Helen sighed as she thought about the story of the bizarre murder, and about Gillian's unending fascination with it. She had refused to gossip with her about it, not because she was lacking information on the subject, but because there was simply too much information to be had. And after the shocking revelations of the past weekend—revelations which had been passed on to her by Jane Emerson, who had in turn heard them from Aggie Binns, the washerwoman in Steep Ride—it seemed there was even more grist for the rumour mill.

In discussion with the investigators, it appeared that the Earl of Yardley had finally disclosed the nature of his business with the Marquis of Sywell on the night he had visited him. It seemed that the Earl had gone to the Abbey to speak to Sywell about his purchasing the Abbey, and apparently, they had agreed—reluctantly on the Earl's part—on a price of two hundred thousand pounds!

Helen had gasped at the staggering sum, as had most of the villagers. To think that the Earl would be willing to pay such an amount of money for something he already owned! But even more astonishing was the Earl's willingness to pay that same amount of money to Sywell's widow. After all, she had had nothing to do with the Marquis's behaviour, the Earl had stated, or with Sywell's reprehensible conduct in acquiring the Abbey in the first place. Why should she not benefit from that which would rightfully have been hers?

That news, of course, had unleashed a flurry of

speculation in the villages. Why was the Earl willing to pay so much money for the Abbey? Was it just a ruse on his part to draw Sywell's widow out of hiding? Many believed it was. Because there were many who believed, like Gillian, that Louise had committed the murder and that she was now in hiding for her life.

Still others believed that the Earl had simply set forward a most generous offer and that Louise would be a foolish young woman indeed not to accept it. And if she were truly innocent of the crime, why would she hesitate to come forward and accept it?

Helen shook her head in confusion, wondering what to make of it all. Certainly, it had become the most widely talked about scandal in years. The girls at Mrs Guarding's Academy were constantly being reprimanded for whispering about it. But even Helen could not deny that it made for diverting conversation. Indeed, she might have tossed it around in her own mind a good deal longer, had she not looked up to see Mr Wymington standing across the road from her. At the sight of the dashing man who had the power to affect both Gillian's future and her own, Helen immediately forgot all about the Marquis and his unfortunate demise. Instead, she took a deep breath, squared her shoulders, and walked forward as calmly as she could to greet him.

'Mr Wymington, thank you for agreeing to see me.'

'I would have been foolish indeed not to meet so beautiful a lady.' Mr Wymington offered her a sweeping bow. 'I take it by Miss Gresham's absence that she is not aware you are seeing me today?'

'No. I thought it best I say what I had to in private.'

'Of course.' He nodded towards the carriage behind

him. 'Would you like to take a drive while we talk or would you prefer to walk?'

Helen glanced at the carriage and shook her head. She was not sure she was comfortable with the idea of being alone in a closed carriage with him. 'Thank you, but it is a lovely day and I think we would do just as well to walk.'

'As you wish, Miss de Coverdale.'

'By the by, how is your uncle?' Helen enquired as she fell into step beside him. 'I do hope he is feeling better.'

'He is much recovered, thank you. But he continues to regret the fact that he was deprived of the pleasure of meeting you and Miss Gresham the other evening.'

A tiny smile pulled at the corner of Helen's mouth. 'I am relieved to hear he is on the mend.'

'Decent of you to say so since you are not even sure he exists. Oh, come, Miss de Coverdale, you must not take offence,' Mr Wymington said when he saw her look of surprise. 'I was aware from the moment of my telling you he was ill that you did not believe he was there. Like Mr Brandon, you are suspicious of my motives with regard to Miss Gresham.'

'You are a man for speaking plainly, Mr Wymington.'

'I am when I feel myself to be with like-minded people.'

'Like-minded?' Helen frowned. 'Why would you consider us to be so?'

'Because you and I were not born as fortunate as some, Miss de Coverdale. We must struggle to make our living, rather than be handed it on a silver platter. You have chosen to seek your rewards by being a schoolmistress, and I through…other means.'

A flutter of anxiety rippled up Helen's spine. 'What other means do you refer to, sir?'

'My dear Miss de Coverdale, I cannot believe you are as naïve as all that. You know full well there are many other avenues for those like us to earn our keep, rather than by hard work alone.'

'Perhaps you should explain yourself, Mr Wymington. I understand that you are at present a half-pay officer in the militia. Are you not content with your station in life?'

'Good God, why should I be?' He laughed harshly. 'The life of an officer is hardly one to be envied. My expenses are always higher than my earnings and I am ill content for them to remain so. I do not apologise for being desirous of a better life.'

'If it is advancement and glory you crave, why not seek a higher commission?'

'Because I haven't the blunt to buy one,' Mr Wymington admitted, his boyish smile evidence of his lack of concern. 'But if I were to marry a wealthy young woman, that would bring about an end to all of my problems, wouldn't it?'

'And I suppose Miss Gresham is the young woman you had in mind?'

'What do you think?'

'I begin to think you are no better than Mr Brandon suspected.'

For a disreputable man, Wymington possessed the smile of an angel. 'No better perhaps, but no worse. I am very fond of Gillian. She is lovely enough to amuse me and has money enough to afford us both a very comfortable life. More importantly, she loves me enough to do whatever I ask.'

'Does that include going against the wishes of her guardian?'

'If necessary. A woman will always choose the man she loves over the parent who raised her. That is the way of the world.'

'You sound very sure of yourself, Mr Wymington,' Helen said coldly. 'Which is surprising, given the circumstances. You must know that I will not allow you to use Gillian in such a manner.'

'And what would you do, fair Helen? Tell her that you have met with me in private and discovered that I really am the scurrilous cad her guardian believes me to be?'

'My name is Miss de Coverdale,' Helen reminded him, 'and why would I not?'

'Because she would not believe you. Oh, I have no doubt she respects you well enough, but she would not take your word over mine. Nor, I think, would she be pleased to hear of our little rendezvous today. I know Mr Brandon would not.'

Helen wasn't in the least surprised by the remark. 'Are you threatening to tell him?'

'If I had to. I am no one's fool, Helen. A man must use whatever means are at his disposal to secure his ends and to ensure his future. It would not be my wish to inform Mr Brandon or Miss Gresham that we had met in secret, but I would do so if I felt it necessary to protect my interests.'

'And what if I told you I intend to tell Mr Brandon about the visit myself?'

'You may tell him whatever you wish. But I suggest you bear in mind the fact that he will not be as angry about our visit today as he will be about the fact that you arranged a secret meeting between Gillian and myself at a deserted cottage.'

It was an undeniable truth, and in light of it Helen fell silent. It seemed her doubts about Sidney Wymington were well founded indeed. He was not above using blackmail to achieve his ends, and if it came right down to it, Helen had no doubt he would twist the truth in any way necessary to make her part in this affair appear as black as his own. The only difference was, he could sway Gillian to his side. She could not. As Wymington had said, Gillian might like and respect her, but if it came to choosing sides, she was far more likely to go with him than with anyone else. Worse still, if Wymington were so inclined, it was very possible he could turn Gillian against all of them.

'Miss Gresham does not turn one-and-twenty for nearly four years,' Helen said quietly. 'In the absence of Mr Brandon's approval to marry, do you really think she will wait for you?'

'She will wait as long as I wish her to,' came Wymington's cocksure reply. 'Once she is back in Hertfordshire, it will be easy enough for me to see her. While she is here, I have only to keep assuring her of my unwavering devotion, which is easy enough to do by sending her the right kind of messages.'

Helen's feelings of concern veered sharply to anger. 'You are not to communicate with her!'

'And how do you intend to stop me, Helen? It is a simple enough matter to get letters to her. You may not be willing to forward my notes, but there are plenty of young ladies at the Academy who are.'

Helen came to an abrupt stop in the middle of the road. She realised now that she had been foolish to think she could persuade this man to give up his quest. Because in doing so, she had jeopardised not only Gillian's future, but her own.

'I think we have said all that needs to be said, Mr Wymington.' Helen's voice was flat, but her eyes flashed with anger and resentment. 'You may threaten me if you wish, but it will do you no good. I *shall* tell Mr Brandon of your conduct. I shall write to him this very day and tell him you are every bit as conniving as he suspected, and that he was right to try to keep you apart. I shall also tell Gillian what kind of man you are, and do everything in my power to change that innocent young girl's opinion of you.'

Mr Wymington breathed a sigh of resignation. 'You may do whatever you wish, my dear Helen. And you are, of course, entitled to your opinions. But in the end, we shall see who comes out ahead. You were wrong to threaten me, my dear. Because I am in a much better position to win than you. A few words in Gillian's ear will rob you of her affection, and a carefully worded note to Mrs Guarding, of your employment. Not that you need have any worry about finding other kinds of work.' Wymington stepped in close and grasped her chin in his hands, tipping it back and forcing her to meet his eyes. 'You are an exceptionally lovely woman. I doubt you would have difficulty in finding a man to take you in. I would set you up as my own mistress, but I doubt you would pleasure me in bed given the way you feel about me now.'

'Hateful man!' Helen jerked her head away. 'How dare you speak to me in such an insolent manner!'

'I am only speaking the truth, my dear. You may enjoy teaching your little girls how to speak the language of love, but we both know that isn't where your true talents lie. You have beauty enough to dazzle any man, and you would be foolish not to make the most of it before it is too late.'

'I will hear no more of this, sir!'

Wymington pretended to be hurt. 'I do wish you would call me Sidney. We are going to be seeing a good deal of each other over the next little while.'

'I will *not* see you again,' Helen said, fighting against the feelings of dread that were even now twisting her stomach into knots. 'Whatever the outcome of this meeting, I shall see to it that you are not allowed to continue in your plan. I will not allow you to ruin that young woman's life.'

Wymington chuckled, but the sound was sly and, at the same time, disturbingly sensual. 'Ruination is not always as bad as it is made out to be, Helen. Gillian may be young, but she longs for adventure and romance, and I can give that to her. Come now; be honest with me. Have you not longed for such adventure in your life? Would you have turned down an opportunity like this, had you found yourself in a similar position at her age?'

His words tore at Helen's heart, and for a moment, she could not speak the words she had to say. She *had* been in a position like this once; hopelessly in love with a man she could not have, and desperate to be with him. So desperate, that when Thomas had suggested they run away together, Helen hadn't even stopped to consider the consequences. She had agreed to an elopement, knowing they would be married as soon as they crossed the Scottish border.

Of course, the elopement had never taken place. Somehow, her father had learned of their plans and had immediately put a stop to them. He'd threatened to go to the Dean with news of Thomas's disgraceful behaviour, and he would have, but for Helen's fevered intervention on his behalf. She had promised her father that if he would let Thomas remain in the church, she would never see him again. And that was exactly what had happened.

But in the months that had followed, Helen had learned just how hard was the task she had set for herself. To live in the same village as the man she loved and to know she could say nothing to him beyond good morning or good afternoon had been torture of the most excruciating kind. But she had not faltered. She had stood by her promise and done everything her father had asked of her. But she could not deny that she *had* been willing to give up everything to be with Thomas.

Was that not exactly what Wymington was talking about now?

Helen took a long, deep breath and then stepped away from him. 'I have nothing more to say to you, Mr Wymington. Other than to advise you that you have made an enemy today.'

'I am sorry to hear that, Helen, but I shall not endeavour to change your mind. I shall only say goodbye until we meet again. And we will meet again.' Mr Wymington bowed, but when he straightened, Helen saw there was nothing of respect in his eyes. 'You can be quite sure of that.'

Chapter Ten

There was only one thought in Helen's mind as she hurried back towards the school. She had to talk to Gillian. She had to convince her that Mr Wymington was a liar and a cheat, and that for her own good, she must never see him again. But how was she to do that? How could she even *begin* such a conversation?

The only way you can begin it, Helen told herself. *By telling Gillian the truth about everything that's happened—including the meeting you had with him today.*

Helen tugged thoughtfully at her bottom lip as she passed through the shadow of Steepwood Abbey. Yes, she would certainly have to reveal what Mr Wymington had said to her, but the question was, would Gillian believe her? She already suspected Helen of siding with Oliver in the matter. Indeed, ever since their visit to Castle Ashby, Gillian had taken to remarking how attentive Oliver had been to her, and how much he seemed to have enjoyed her company.

Naturally, Helen had been quick to deny it. She

has assured Gillian that Mr Brandon had merely been playing the part of an attentive host, and when reminded of the amount of time they had spent alone together, had replied that neither she nor Mr Brandon had wished to intrude on the good time the two girls seemed to be having.

Gillian hadn't believed a word of it, of course. And judging by the complacent smile she'd given Helen, the girl had formed her own impressions as to what was going on between her guardian and her teacher. In which case, Helen knew there was very little chance of Gillian believing her in this.

It did not make for an enviable situation, and when Helen got up the next morning she was no closer to knowing how to resolve matters than she had been when she'd gone to bed. She continued to think about it throughout the day, but had still not reached a decision when they set off for church on Sunday morning. Unfortunately, matters quickly went downhill and in a manner Helen couldn't even have begun to anticipate.

It all started when Oliver showed up unexpectedly after the service and invited Gillian and Helen to join him for a drive.

'Oh, Oliver, how splendid of you to suggest it,' Gillian exclaimed. 'I should love to go for a drive, and I'm sure Miss de Coverdale would too.' She slid a knowing glance towards her teacher. 'After all, the two of you got along so well at Castle Ashby.'

Helen felt her face go three shades of red. 'Thank you, Miss Gresham, but I do not think my joining you today would be appropriate.'

'Of course it would,' Gillian said, refusing to be denied. 'It will be far more pleasant than returning

to school. Will you treat us to some refreshments as
well, Oliver?'

'I think that could be arranged.'

'In that case, I shall certainly not join you,' Helen
said quickly.

'Do you not eat, Miss de Coverdale?' Oliver enquired, a twinkle forming in his eyes.

'I do, sir, but not at someone else's expense.'

'Excuse me, Miss de Coverdale?'

Helen turned as Sally Jenkins came running up to
her. 'Yes, Miss Jenkins, what is it?'

'Pardon the interruption, miss, but I was told to
give you this.'

Helen glanced down at the small package Sally
was holding out to her and frowned. 'What is it?'

'I don't know, miss. The gentleman said I was to
give it to you as soon as you came out of church.'

'What gentleman?'

'Mr Wymington, miss.'

Helen heard Gillian's sharp gasp of dismay beside
her, but it was Oliver's reaction she feared the most.
She glanced up at him to see his smile disappear and
an expression of disbelief settle upon his features.
'Wymington is *here*?'

'I d-don't know. Miss Jenkins, did the gentleman
say his name was…Mr Wymington?'

'Yes, Miss. He made me repeat it twice so I
wouldn't forget.'

'But…where did you see him?'

'Over by the commons. He told me I was to give
this to you because you had left it in his carriage.'

'In his *carriage*?' Gillian's expression reflected
her feelings of shock and dismay. 'But…when were
you in Mr Wymington's carriage?'

'I wasn't.' Helen's heart raced as she stared at the package in her hand. 'I have no idea what this is all about.'

'But you have *seen* Mr Wymington?'

That question came from Oliver and there was no mistaking the tone of voice. Helen looked up, and shivered at the iciness of his gaze. 'Mr Brandon, I think it would be best if we discussed this in private—'

'I asked you a question, Miss de Coverdale. Have you seen Mr Wymington in or around Steep Abbot?'

Helen sighed, painfully aware there was nothing she could do but tell him the truth. 'Yes. I arranged to meet with him on…Friday afternoon in Abbot Giles.'

'You *arranged* to meet him?' Gillian echoed in disbelief. 'But I don't understand. Why would you wish to do such a thing?'

'Perhaps before you answer that, you should open the box and see what Mr Wymington has returned to you,' Oliver said in a cold, disapproving voice.

Helen risked a quick look at Gillian, saw the doubt and bewilderment in her eyes, and then glanced down at the package. She folded back the paper with fingers that were visibly trembling, and to her astonishment, found herself staring at one of her new kid gloves.

'That is your glove, Miss de Coverdale,' Gillian exclaimed. 'I have seen you wear it on several occasions.'

Helen stared at it in bafflement. It certainly *looked* like her glove, but how could Mr Wymington possibly have gained possession of it? She hadn't left it in the cottage the afternoon she and Gillian had gone to see him, nor had she taken it off when she had met him in Abbot Giles.

'It is one very much like it, I admit, but I…cannot be sure it is the same.'

Oliver picked up the glove and examined it. 'Where did you get these gloves, Miss de Coverdale?'

'A very good friend sent them to me.'

'From London?'

'Yes.'

Oliver nodded. 'I know the shop where they are made. The workmanship is quite distinctive and they do not come cheap. Gloves like these would not be common property around here. I can only assume it would have to be yours.'

'But there is no way Mr Wymington could have come into possession of it.'

'Why not? Were you wearing them when you met him in Abbot Giles?'

'Yes, but I did not take them off. And it is impossible for me to have left it in Mr Wymington's carriage, because I have never *been* in his carriage.'

'Why then would he say you had?' Gillian demanded.

Searching her mind for a plausible explanation, Helen could only shake her head in dismay. Something warned her that Wymington had planned this. He'd wanted her to be humiliated in front of Gillian. He had wanted to discredit her, and to make her look deceitful, and he had more than succeeded.

'Go back to school with Miss Brookwell and wait for me there, Gillian,' Oliver said abruptly.

'But Oliver—'

'Do as I say, child. I wish to speak to Miss de Coverdale alone.'

Looking very unhappy and more than a little confused, Gillian turned and slowly walked away. She glanced back over her shoulder a few times, her face a study in dejection as she looked from one to the other of them.

Oliver waited until she was well beyond their hearing before he turned to Helen and said, 'Now, Miss de Coverdale, would you care to explain what this is all about?'

Awkwardly, Helen cleared her throat. 'Truly, sir, I have no idea—'

'Pray do not take me for a fool, Miss de Coverdale.' Oliver's expression darkened ominously. 'Whether or not this *is* your glove is hardly the issue here. What is, is that you have been in contact with Sidney Wymington, and that you have chosen not to tell me about it.'

'But I have a good explanation—'

'If there is an explanation, I doubt it will be good,' Oliver snapped. 'Since you said you had *arranged* to meet Wymington, I can only assume you knew what he looked like. Does that mean you had occasion to see him prior to your Friday afternoon meeting in Abbot Giles?'

Reluctantly, Helen nodded. 'Yes, but—'

'And was Gillian with you?'

At that, Helen stopped. She didn't dare tell him that she had taken Gillian to see Mr Wymington in Abbot Quincey. Not without explaining why. But surely she could reveal the details of their chance encounter on the road. Surely he would not hold her culpable for that. 'Yes she was. Mr Wymington happened to come upon us as we were walking home from church.'

Sparks danced in Oliver's eyes. 'Did you not think that a little strange given that Mr Wymington resides in Hertfordshire?'

Helen's temper began to flare. 'Of course I did.'

'Yet on the strength of that meeting, you arranged to meet him again in Abbot Giles?'

'Well, no, not precisely.'

'Not precisely?'

Helen closed her eyes. It seemed that with every word, she was digging herself deeper into a hole. 'I arranged to see him again…after I had met with him at his uncle's cottage in Abbot Quincey.'

For a moment, there was complete silence. Then, like a volcano, Oliver's anger began to erupt. 'You met with him in the privacy of a family member's home?'

'Mr Brandon, I can assure you—'

'I want no assurances, Miss de Coverdale, other than to be told that Gillian did *not* accompany you on that visit.'

'I fear I really must be allowed to speak—'

'Damn and blast it, woman, answer my question! Did Gillian go with you when you went to see Wymington?'

Helen cringed at the anger in his voice. 'Yes, but if you would just let me explain—'

'No! I will hear no more! I let it be known in no uncertain terms, that Gillian was not to be allowed *any* contact with Mr Wymington, and yet today I learn that not only have you been in contact with him, but that you have exposed Gillian to him as

well. Well that is not satisfactory, Miss de Coverdale. By God, it is not!'

A very short time later, Oliver jerked the horses
to a halt in front of Mrs Guarding's Academy. 'Has
Mrs Guarding returned from church?' he demanded
of the young lad who came running to hold the
horses.

'Aye, sir. A few minutes ago.'

'Good.' He tossed the reins to the boy, ordered
him to hold them until he returned, and then, taking
the stone steps two at a time, flung open the front
door and climbed the stairs to the headmistress's sitting-room. He barely waited for an answer to his
knock before he opened the door and walked in.

'Mrs Guarding, I have come to express my extreme dissatisfaction with you and a member of your
staff.'

The smile of welcome that had been forming on
the headmistress's face died within seconds of his
greeting. 'Mr Brandon, whatever has happened?'

'Only that which I tried to prevent by warning you
well in advance of its likelihood.'

'Would you care to sit down?'

'I am far too agitated to sit, madam.' Oliver began
to pace the length of the room. 'I have just learned
that my ward has been in contact with Sidney
Wymington, and that Miss de Coverdale had a hand
in the meeting taking place.'

'Miss de Coverdale?' The headmistress's disbelief
was plain. 'I am sure there must be some mistake. I
cannot believe Helen would do such a thing.'

'I regret to inform you that she has. I have just
learned of the entire sorry affair. I thought to take

Gillian and Miss de Coverdale for a drive, but whilst talking to them, a package was delivered to Miss de Coverdale by one of the students. It seems she left one of her gloves in Mr Wymington's carriage.'

Mrs Guarding gasped softly, and then leaned against the corner of her desk. 'Are you sure it was her glove?'

'I don't give a damn if it was.' Oliver's voice was cold and deliberate. 'The fact is, she has seen the man on three different occasions, the most recent of which was a meeting that she arranged herself in a nearby village. But far more distressing to me is the fact that she has allowed Gillian to be in contact with him as well.'

By now, Mrs Guarding's face had gone ashen. 'Mr Brandon, I really have no idea what to say.'

'There is nothing to say, madam,' Oliver interrupted harshly. 'I put my trust in you to keep Gillian safe from that man, only to discover that my faith has been sorely misplaced. Especially in regard to Miss de Coverdale. I begin to wonder if everything she's told me has been a Banbury tale.'

'Mr Brandon, I can understand your being angry. And while I have no idea what has transpired here, I do intend to find out. But you have no reason to doubt that anything else Miss de Coverdale has told you is anything but the truth.'

'Good God, madam, do you really expect me to believe that?' Oliver's laugh exploded as a harsh burst of sound. 'The woman went behind my back and did *exactly* what I asked her not to. She knew how I felt about Mr Wymington, yet she wilfully allowed this abominable meeting to take place. Well, that is not acceptable. I demand you take measures to remedy the situation at once.'

Mrs Guarding nodded, but her eyes were deeply troubled. 'Yes, of course. I shall speak to her at immediately upon her return.'

'I expect you to do more than speak to her, Mrs Guarding. I want Miss de Coverdale dismissed. If she is not, I shall ensure that no young lady of quality ever sets foot in this establishment again. Furthermore, I intend to remove Gillian before the end of the month and take her back to Hertfordshire, where with any luck, I shall find a suitable young man willing to marry her.' Oliver turned on his heel and headed for the door. 'Business matters compel me to leave first thing in the morning, but I shall stay at the Angel for the night. You may let me know of your decision there.'

Helen did not see Oliver again that afternoon. She knew he had spoken to Mrs Guarding, and she assumed he would talk to Gillian, but beyond that she had no idea of what he was planning to do. She sat on the edge of the bed in her tiny room and picked up the letter that had been waiting for her upon her return from church. With a heavy heart, she read the damning words again.

Dear Helen

I trust Miss Gresham and Mr Brandon were suitably impressed by the gallant return of your misplaced glove. A simple gesture, I thought, but highly effective. You are no match for me, my dear. You would do well to remember that. SCW

This, then, was what Mr Wymington had referred to when he'd said he would do whatever was necessary to achieve his goal. The entire performance had been planned with a view to discrediting her in front of Gillian. Obviously, he had convinced one of the girls—with heaven knew *what* kind of trickery— to remove the glove from her room and to bring it to him. Certainly, he had timed the delivery of it well. He knew that she and Gillian would be together after church and by making sure that the glove was delivered to her in such a way, it would have been obvious to Gillian that they had met. The fact that Oliver had been there to witness her disgrace had been an unexpected bonus.

Helen tried to ignore the tearing pain in her chest as she thought about Oliver and the way he had reacted. Would she ever forget the way he had looked at her when she had mentioned Mr Wymington's name? Would she ever be able to banish the memory of the disappointment and anger that had appeared in his eyes during the conversation that had followed?

She feared not. She hadn't realised until that moment just how much his good opinion had meant to her. She had been so pleased when they had been able to resolve their differences from the past. And she had enjoyed, more than she cared to admit, the time she had spent with him at Castle Ashby.

But all of that was gone now. She had done something she'd known all along to be wrong, and had lost not only his respect but her own credibility. Even now, he would be questioning the validity of everything she had told him. He might even begin to believe she *had* invited Lord Talbot's advances, regardless of what the drunken peer had admitted to. And what about Mrs Guarding? What would she do if the headmistress turned her away?

Helen's face crumpled. After all, she had blatantly disregarded the rules. She had ignored her instructions and had taken matters into her own hands. What choice would the headmistress have but to turn her away?

When a tentative knock came at the door, Helen froze. 'Yes?'

'Miss de Coverdale?'

Helen gasped, and quickly opened the door. 'Gillian, what are you doing here?'

'I had to see you.' The girl walked in and collapsed on the bed. 'Oliver is furious.'

'Yes, I'd expected as much. Did he scold you very badly?'

Gillian's bottom lip trembled. 'He didn't say much to me at all. I don't think he could find the words. But I am terribly afraid he is going to take me away.'

There was such a plaintive quality to the girl's voice that it nearly broke Helen's heart. 'Oh, Gillian, I am so sorry.'

'Why did you have to tell him I had been in contact with Mr Wymington? He would never have found out if you hadn't.'

'I could not lie to him, Gillian. It was bad enough we did something without his knowledge. To compound that by lying would have made it even worse. Besides, he already knew I had seen Mr Wymington myself.'

'But *why* did you arrange to see Mr Wymington in Abbot Giles?'

Helen had been expecting the question, but somehow, it didn't make the answering of it any easier. 'Because I was…troubled by something he'd said to me when we were leaving his uncle's cottage.'

'Why? What did he say?'

Helen wished there was some way she could soften the blow Gillian was about to receive, but she knew in her heart there was not. 'Gillian, Mr Wymington hasn't been completely honest with you about his feelings.'

Gillian went very still. 'What do you mean?'

'I mean that your guardian has been right all along. Mr Wymington admitted to me that…the reason he is courting you is because he is interested in securing a wealthy bride.'

'*No!*'

'I wish I could say it wasn't so—'

'No, it isn't true!' Gillian sprang to her feet, her blue eyes blazing with anger. 'You are only saying that to make me *think* he doesn't love me. But he *does* love me! He told me so himself!'

'Mr Wymington would tell you whatever he thought he had to to make you believe him, Gillian, don't you see that?' Helen took the girl by the shoulders and gave her a gentle shake. 'He's not a wealthy man, but he knows that by marrying you he will become one.'

'But the money is mine!'

'Yes, but when a woman marries, everything she owns becomes the property of her husband. You would have absolutely no say in how your money was spent, or on what.'

Suddenly, Gillian jerked free of Helen's hands. 'You like him, don't you!'

Helen blanched. '*What?*'

'You like Mr Wymington,' she repeated. 'That's why you went to see him, isn't it?'

Helen flinched at the accusation in Gillian's voice. 'Of course it isn't. What nonsense!'

But Gillian only shook her head and began to back towards the door. 'No, it isn't nonsense. He told me you would say terrible things like this. He told me you would…try to make me think badly of him, because you were jealous and wanted him for yourself. But I didn't believe it.' Gillian looked at her with a haunted expression. 'I didn't *want* to believe it.'

'Gillian, what do you mean he *told* you that's what I would say? Have you been in contact with him?'

'That's none of your concern,' Gillian cried.

'Yes, Gillian, it is. Have you had a letter from him?'

'All right, yes, I have!' Her tone was defiant. 'And I want the others he sent to you for me. You had no right to keep them! They were mine!'

Stunned, Helen rocked back on her heels. Dear God, how could everything have gone so terribly, terribly wrong? 'Gillian, listen to me. Mr Wymington had no business sending you letters. He was wrong to try to contact you, and he was certainly wrong to try to do it through me. Mr Brandon expressly forbade any correspondence between the two of you.'

'I do not think that is the case at all,' Gillian said, her voice ringing with condemnation. 'You like Mr Wymington and you didn't like the idea of his sending letters to me.'

'That is utterly ridiculous!'

'No, it isn't. Mr Wymington is a wonderful man! Any woman would be proud to have him by her side.

And you're just an old spinster who can't find a gentleman of her own,' Gillian flung at her. 'That's why you tried to take mine.'

Helen gasped at the cruelty of the indictment. 'I would never do such a thing!'

'Yes, you would. Well, I hope Mrs Guarding does dismiss you!' Gillian said as she threw open the door. 'I hope she sends you away as soon as possible. Because I never ever want to see you again!'

Chapter Eleven

Mrs Guarding sent for her thirty minutes later.

Helen went to the headmistress's office with a heavy heart. Her world was falling apart and there was absolutely nothing she could do to stop it. First Oliver had turned against her, then Gillian, and now, she was to be taken to task by Mrs Guarding. Would this wretched day never end?

'So you were, in fact, a willing accomplice to the meeting between Gillian and Mr Wymington,' Mrs Guarding said at the end of Helen's recounting of the events.

'Only in that I allowed it to take place.' Helen breathed a heavy sigh. 'I had to know if Mr Wymington was truly as reprehensible as Mr Brandon believed him to be. I thought that by going and listening to his conversation with Miss Gresham, I might be able to discover something about him which would confirm Mr Brandon's suspicions.'

'Which you did.'

'Yes.'

'And that is why you arranged to meet with him again in Abbot Giles,' Mrs Guarding said slowly.

'I know you think I was inclined to disbelieve Mr Brandon because of my past, Mrs Guarding, but I had to find out the truth. I thought that if I could go to Gillian with proof of Mr Wymington's duplicity, she would be able to see that her guardian was right.'

'And yet, in spite of what you were able to learn about Mr Wymington, Gillian is enamoured of him still.'

Helen's head fell forward in despair. 'Yes.'

Mrs Guarding got up and slowly began to walk around the room. 'You say that Gillian and Mr Wymington have been exchanging letters.'

'I can only assume that some of the girls have been helping the messages go back and forth. Mr Wymington was not above using trinkets or sweets to encourage them, and indeed, the girls would have no reason to believe they were doing anything wrong. It was only the staff that were told there was to be no communication allowed. No doubt the girls thought it all very romantic. A kind of Romeo and Juliet relationship, as it were.'

'Hmm, and look where love got *them*,' Mrs Guarding muttered. 'Well, we are in a fine mess, my dear. Mr Brandon has threatened the future of the school if I do not dismiss you, yet your reasons for doing what you did—if not the manner in which you did them—are only to be commended. Especially in light of Mr Wymington's true nature. Unfortunately, I am once again caught in the middle of the problem, forced to choose between what I feel to be right and what is best for the school.'

Helen closed her eyes. 'I am so very sorry, Mrs Guarding. I had no idea it would come to this.

Certainly, it was never my wish to cause you so much aggravation.'

'I know, my dear, but unfortunately, being sorry doesn't make the problem go away.' Mrs Guarding sighed again. 'Go back to your room, Helen. I shall take the evening to think the matter over and advise you and Mr Brandon of my decision in the morning.'

'Has Mr Brandon returned to Hertfordshire?'

'No. He has taken a room at the Angel, but he has asked for my decision before he leaves in the morning. Did I mention that he has also advised me of his intention to remove Gillian from the school?'

Helen gasped. 'No!'

'I believe he intends to settle her in marriage as soon as possible.'

With every word, Helen's spirits plummeted even further. 'She will hate that above all. I wonder she did not mention it to me.'

'I am not sure she knows. Mr Brandon possibly would not wish to upset her to the point where she might do something foolish before he can get her home.'

That made sense, Helen reflected sadly. Oliver didn't trust Gillian at the best of times. In the state she was in now, there was no telling *what* she might do.

'By the way, it would probably be best if you did not see Gillian until I've made my decision,' Mrs Guarding advised. 'No doubt she will be feeling extremely troubled by all that has happened.'

Helen remembered the acrimonious tone of the girl's voice; the stinging words of condemnation she had thrown at her, and regretfully nodded her head.

'Yes, I have no doubt that she is, at the moment, a very troubled young lady indeed.'

Helen went back to her room and thought long and hard about the situation she found herself in. And the more she thought about it, the more she realised it was not only her future that was at stake here, but Gillian's. The child had to be kept safe from the likes of Sidney Wymington, but how? Wymington certainly couldn't be trusted to keep *his* distance. Events of the past few weeks were evidence of that. And knowing the man as well as she did, Helen was convinced he would do everything in his power to continue his clandestine courtship.

But was Oliver's intention of taking her back to Hertfordshire and settling her in a marriage of convenience the right answer? He would no doubt choose someone respectable. An older man, perhaps; someone who was steady and reliable, and who would have a settling effect on Gillian. But Gillian was in a highly emotional state right now. How would she react to Oliver choosing a husband for her and *forcing* her into marriage? '…How can he know what is best for me when he has never been in love himself?' Gillian had complained. 'How can he know how sweet it is to be close to someone you love when he has never experienced the feeling himself?'

There was no need for Helen to try to answer the question. Oliver's intervention in such a way would surely bring about the end of his relationship with his ward. If Gillian could not choose the man she would spend the rest of her life with, she might very well choose never to see Oliver again!

* * *

Oliver was sitting in his room, contemplating his problems over a bottle of claret, when he heard the sound of heavy footsteps in the hallway beyond.

'Mr Brandon?' the innkeeper called through the door.

Oliver didn't bother to get up. 'What is it?'

'Pardon me, sir, but there's a young lady downstairs asking to have a word with you.'

Oliver frowned. A young lady? At this time of night? Obviously not the kind of young lady he was interested in seeing. 'Tell her I've already gone to bed,' he called back gruffly.

'She said to tell you she was from the school, sir.'

The school? Good heavens, had Gillian come to see him?

Oliver jumped to his feet and shrugged on his jacket. 'Innkeeper, have you a decent parlour downstairs?'

'Aye, sir.'

'Good. Put the young lady in it and tell her I shall be there directly.'

As Oliver prepared to go downstairs, he wondered why Gillian had come. Was it possible she wished to apologise for her conduct? She certainly hadn't seemed inclined to do so this afternoon. Of course, she'd had a few hours to think things over. Mayhaps she had seen the folly of her ways and was hoping to make amends.

To his astonishment, however, it wasn't his disobedient young ward who awaited him in the privacy of the parlour. Instead, as the young woman slipped back the hood of her cape, Oliver was treated to the sight of the woman who had caused him an endless number of sleepless nights and an even greater number of disturbing dreams. 'Miss de Coverdale!'

'Pray forgive my calling upon you at so late an hour, Mr Brandon, but it was imperative that I speak with you.'

'Have you no care for your reputation?'

'I have little enough reputation left to worry about,' Helen said. 'I felt that what I had to say was worth the risks in coming.'

It took a moment for Oliver to gather his wits about him. Damn it, why did the mere sight of her cause his insides to turn to liquid? 'I thought Gillian had come to pay a call,' he said huskily. 'Had I known it was you, I would not have agreed to a meeting.'

Helen flushed at the harshness of the rebuke. 'I know. That is why I did not give the innkeeper my name. But I had to come, sir. I had to talk to you about Gillian's future.'

Oliver's eyes darkened. 'It seems to me you should be more concerned with your own, Miss de Coverdale. I am sure Mrs Guarding informed you of my ultimatum.'

'She did, and I shall deal with that at the proper time. But how you deal with Gillian's future is far more important to me right now.' Helen took a hesitant step forward. 'Mr Brandon, is it your intention to take Gillian back to Hertfordshire and settle her in an arranged marriage?'

'I fail to see that what I do with my ward is any business of yours.'

'Oh, but it is, sir. Because I fear that what you are about to do is a terrible mistake. Gillian puts a greater value on love than she does on anything else. Indeed, she believes it to be the most important thing in the world.'

'Unfortunately, you and I have both seen what happens when Gillian puts that much stock in love,' Oliver drawled. 'And I think it should be obvious why I would not wish to see her make her own decision again.' He turned and walked towards the window. Why was this so damned difficult? Why couldn't he just be angry with her and stay that way? 'Why did you go against my wishes and allow her to see Wymington?' he asked softly. 'You knew better than anyone how I felt about the man.'

'Yes, but I had to see for myself what Mr Wymington was like.'

'Why would you think to question my own assessment of the man?'

'Because I could not be sure that your reasons for disliking him were sound.'

Oliver whirled to face her, and his expression was a study in anger. 'Do you think I am completely insensitive, Miss de Coverdale, or just supremely stupid?'

Helen flushed, but valiantly held her ground. 'I think that, as Gillian's stepbrother and guardian, you might have been jealous that she was giving her affections so completely to someone else. To listen to Gillian speak of him, Mr Wymington is a paragon amongst men.'

Oliver gave a short burst of frustrated laughter. 'I have had the acquaintance of many men, Miss de Coverdale, and I have yet to meet a paragon. However, I do not expect Gillian to have a great deal of sense when it comes to matters like this. She is young and foolish, and has been indulged far more than she ought. But I do expect those in my employ, and those in whom I put my trust to abide by my wishes. You have not. And however justifiable you feel your actions to be, it still does not change the fact that you deliberately disobeyed me.' He turned back towards the window, and his voice dropped away. 'I trusted you, Miss de Coverdale. I believed you to be a good influence on Gillian. I knew how much she respected you and as I came to know you better, I felt that same respect myself. Indeed, I agonised over the mistake I had made in believing you to be…something you were not,' he said quietly. 'And yet, what did I discover today but that you are not to be trusted at all.'

Helen blinked as a soft shimmer of tears appeared in her eyes. 'Mr Brandon, I know there is nothing I can say to excuse my own conduct, but I did not come here to plead my case. I came here to talk to you about Gillian's.' She took a tentative step closer. 'Is it your intention to find Gillian a husband without her knowledge or consent?'

Oliver was silent for a moment, his eyes fixed on the deserted street below. Did she truly care so little about her own predicament that she would not even seek his forgiveness? 'Yes, it is.' His voice was flat, his tone lacking in emotion. 'It is clear that Gillian wishes to be married, so the sooner I settle her in the wedded state, the better off we shall all be.'

'She will resent your intrusion into her life,' Helen said quietly. 'Gillian needs to be in love with the man she marries. She will suffocate in a relationship that exists in name only.'

'We have already agreed that people marry for reasons other than love, Miss de Coverdale,' Oliver replied in the same, bland tone. 'Gillian needs guidance in her life. She needs the firm hand of a husband to tell her what she can and cannot do. And since I cannot trust her to find the kind of man who will do that, I shall have to do it for her.'

His words fell into the heavy silence between them; a silence broken only by the faint sputtering of the candle on the table.

'Mr Brandon, you told Mrs Guarding that you…wanted my resignation. If I agreed to leave the school, would you consider allowing Gillian to stay?'

Oliver sighed, and then slowly turned to look at her. She was such a beautiful woman. In the dim light of the candle, her loveliness seemed to him almost ethereal. He gazed in silence at the gentle oval of her face and at the long, dark hair falling in glistening waves past her shoulders. His eyes lingered for a moment on the inviting curve of her mouth and upon the ripe fullness of her lips. And he knew that, had it been possible, he would have done anything he could to banish the expression of fear and uncertainty from her eyes.

But he could not. He could not back down from the stance he had taken. And in acknowledging that, he also acknowledged that, after tonight, he would never see Helen again.

'I do not see that leaving Gillian at Guarding's will serve any useful purpose.' Oliver's voice was firm, yet tinged with regret. 'Mr Wymington has been able to see her and to correspond with her easily enough during the past two months. What makes you think he would stop just because you were no longer there?'

It was, Helen supposed, a logical answer. Until Gillian made up her own mind not to see Mr

Wymington, there would be little anyone could do to stop her. Which meant, she realised sadly, that there was nothing more she could do here.

'Mr Brandon, I deeply regret the disappointment I have caused you. I care about Gillian, and would hate to see her throw herself away on a man like Wymington. But I fear that in my efforts to help, I have managed only to exacerbate the situation, and for that I am truly sorry. It was not my wish to make things more difficult for you than they already were.'

Oliver gazed across the room at her, and was seized by a sudden, inexplicable longing to take her in his arms and hold her close. He wished he could make the suffering he saw so plainly etched upon her face go away, for in truth, he knew how deeply she cared for his ward. He knew that what she had done, she had done with the girl's best interests at heart. But still something held him back. The knowledge that Helen had betrayed his trust by going against his wishes would not allow him to take that step forward. For while he could accept that her heart had been in the right place, he still could not bring himself to accept that she had deceived him.

'What do you intend to do now, Miss de Coverdale?' he asked.

Helen offered him a half-hearted smile. 'Mrs Guarding has told me that she will give me her decision in the morning. I shall make my own then. For now, I shall take up no more of your time.' She drew the hood up over her head and started for the door. 'Thank you for listening to me, Mr Brandon.'

'Shall I walk you back to the school?' Oliver asked, taking an unconscious step towards her.

Helen quickly shook her head, her eyes suspiciously bright. 'Thank you, but I know the way. Goodnight, Mr Brandon.'

As the door closed behind her, Oliver closed his eyes and drew an unsteady breath. 'Goodnight, my dear Helen,' he whispered into the silence. 'And...goodbye.'

Long before the sun rose to brighten the morning sky, Helen knew what she had to do. She had lain awake most of the night, restlessly tossing and turning as she reviewed in painful detail the events of the past week. And after considering all of the options, she settled on the only one that she felt suitable to resolving the situation.

She sat down at her desk and wrote out two letters. She did not stop to consider her own feelings as her pen flew across the paper. She knew in her heart that what she was doing was right, because this wasn't about her. It was about doing what she had to for the people she loved.

Her first letter was to Mrs Guarding. In it, she thanked the headmistress for being such a faithful ally, and expressed at length her gratitude for having had the opportunity to be a part of the Guarding Academy for Girls. She then went on to say that, given what was at stake, she felt it best that she resign her position and leave the school as quickly as possible. That way, Mr Brandon's demands would be met and hopefully, it would ensure that any plans for future retribution would be set aside. He might even be persuaded to reconsider his position and allow Gillian to remain at the school.

Helen's second letter was to Oliver, and it was considerably more difficult to write. Her feelings for him had only deepened in the past weeks, and she knew that she had fallen in love with him. It was foolish, yes, but she had long since given up believing that anything to do with love was logical. Unfortunately, she also recognised that the way she felt about him could have no bearing on what she had to say. Because this too, had to be done for the best of all concerned.

Helen sealed the two letters and then quickly took them down to the kitchen. She gave Oliver's letter to one of the young lads with instructions to deliver it to the Angel, and then slid the other one under Mrs Guarding's sitting-room door. Then, returning to her room, she began her preparations for the day to come.

She had learned to live without the love of a man once in her life. Surely she could learn to do it again.

Helen's letter was delivered to Oliver just as he was preparing to leave. He read it over slowly, a deep groove appearing in his forehead as he realised what she was saying.

Dear Mr Brandon

I am sure it will come as no surprise to you that I have tendered my resignation to Mrs Guarding. I should have accepted your instructions without question, and I regret that my desire to do good has caused so much heartache. I can, however, assure you that your suspicions with regards to Mr Wymington are correct.

The gentleman freely admitted to me that his interest in your ward was largely financial, and that he is convinced of his power over her; a power I believe he will not hesitate to use. In that, I can agree with your wish to remove Miss Gresham to Hertfordshire as soon as possible. But I would advise you to be cautious even there, for I am not convinced that he will so easily give up his pursuit.

I would ask only one thing of you, sir. That is, that you reconsider your decision to force Gillian into a marriage of convenience. I cannot stress how detrimental I feel this would be, both to her, and to your continuing relationship with her. Gillian believes that love is the most important thing in the world, and as a result, her view of marriage is somewhat idealistic. I would suggest that if she is to be married, let it be to someone of her own choosing. She is far more likely to forget Mr Wymington if the gentleman who takes his place is one for whom she can feel genuine affection, rather than someone for whom she feels nothing.

Again, please accept my heartfelt apologies for the problems I have caused.

> Yours most sincerely,
> Helen de Coverdale

Oliver sighed. So, she had resigned. Good. That was what he'd wanted, wasn't it? After all, if teachers and servants were allowed to take matters into their own hands, the result would be social anarchy. There had to be some control exercised over their conduct.

But if that was the case, why did he feel so damned wretched about the entire affair?

Oliver tossed the letter on to the bed and slowly walked around the room. What would Helen do now? Go back into service? He thought it likely. But this time, she would hardly do so with a letter of recommendation to ease her way. Mrs Guarding would not be able to provide her with one, given the circumstances under which she was leaving.

Which meant that Helen would have no choice but to seek a lesser position in a large house, perhaps as a lady's maid or a companion. He doubted she would wish to serve as a governess again. A woman so beautiful would never truly be safe in any man's house.

Oddly enough, Oliver didn't like to think of Helen in such a position. He could not bear the thought of her having to fight for her virtue against men like Lord Talbot, or even Sidney Wymington. Of course, why he'd give a damn about what other men did to her made absolutely no sense at all. She was nothing to him.

So why should the idea of another man making love to her make him want to run out and do everything he could to stop it from happening?

Reluctantly, Mrs Guarding accepted Helen's resignation.

'What will you do now, Helen?' she asked as she slowly folded up the letter.

Helen tried to put a brave face on the situation. 'I'm not sure. Perhaps I shall apply to a domestic agency for work. I thought perhaps a position as a companion might be suitable.'

'You would not consider going into service as a governess again?'

'Not as long as there is anything else I can do, no.'

Mrs Guarding nodded. 'I suppose I can understand your feeling that way, given everything that's happened. But I am so very sorry to lose you, Helen.'

Helen nodded tightly. 'I am very sorry to be going.'

'I will, of course, prepare a letter of recommendation for you. Hopefully it will make matters easier.'

Helen stared at the headmistress in astonishment. 'You would do that for me? But…I don't understand. You were not able to give Desirée such a letter.'

'No, because her situation was not the same as yours. In Desirée's case, there were witnesses to the incident with Lord Perry. Here, the evidence is strictly circumstantial, and you yourself were not involved in any act of impropriety. I fail to see why you should be penalised for trying to help Miss Gresham, simply because it was not in the accepted way.'

Helen gulped hard, hoping the older woman would not see how close to tears she really was. 'You are…too kind, Mrs Guarding. I had not expected such charity, given everything I have done.'

'It grieves me to see you leave under conditions like this,' the headmistress admitted, her own voice brusque. 'Nor am I entirely pleased with Mr Brandon's decision to take Gillian back to Hertfordshire, now that you have sacrificed your position here.'

Helen smiled faintly. 'Thank you, but my being here has nothing to do with his decision. He would have done that whether I stayed or not. No, it is his plan to settle Gillian in a marriage of convenience that causes me the greatest concern. Because I truly believe that, in the long run, *that* will be the straw that breaks the proverbial camel's back.'

Chapter Twelve

October, 1812

In the drawing room at Shefferton Hall, Sophie regarded her brother with an expression of doubt and concern. 'Are you sure there is nothing else to be done, Oliver? It seems a rather drastic measure.'

'Drastic it may be but I fear it is our only choice.' Oliver stood with his back to her and stared through the window into the darkness. 'I want you to find Gillian a husband by Christmas.'

'That does not give us much time.'

'It need not take much time. You must know of an eligible gentleman who is looking for a wife.'

'Well, yes, but not necessarily one of whom Gillian will approve.'

'I do not intend to study Gillian's wishes in the matter.' Oliver's voice was terse. 'She cannot be trusted to use her head in choosing a husband, so we must use ours. And I will tolerate no interference from anyone in this.'

'If you are referring to Miss de Coverdale, I think

you are being unnecessarily harsh, Oliver,' Sophie observed. 'It seems to me the woman was only trying to help.'

Oliver's face stiffened. 'I do not wish to discuss Miss de Coverdale's participation in this, Sophie. I gave explicit instructions beforehand and I expected them to be obeyed.'

'Yes, but by not doing so, Miss de Coverdale has given you proof of Mr Wymington's deceitfulness. Proof you yourself said you were in need of.'

'Proof it may be, but it has done little to change Gillian's mind. She is still of the opinion that the man is a paragon.' Oliver all but spat the word. 'That is why I want her here at Shefferton, where I can keep my eye on her. At least until she is safely married.'

It was clear from the expression on Sophie's face that she was far from happy, but as though sensing it would be impossible to change her brother's mind, she merely lifted her shoulders in a graceful shrug. 'Very well, if this is what you wish, I will see what I can find out.' She stopped and thought for a moment. 'There is young Nigel Riddleston, I suppose.'

Oliver turned. 'The baronet's son?'

'Yes. He is a pleasant young man. Perhaps not as dashing as Mr Wymington, but he is certainly handsome enough. And if I do not miss my guess, he has been harbouring a tendre for Gillian ever since Lady Tingley's musicale last summer.'

Oliver slowly nodded his head. Yes, he knew the lad. He was a good-natured chap with a keen wit and a well-grounded sense of duty and obligation. And there was both money and property in the family. Yes, he might be just the man, Oliver thought with relief. Hopefully, in time, Gillian would come to love him. For while Oliver was loathe to commit his step-sister to a loveless marriage, he was determined to protect her from the Sidney Wymingtons of the world.

'Thank you, Sophie. If you would be so good as to meet with Mr Riddleston and see if there is any interest on his part, I shall begin to prepare Gillian.'

Sophie glanced towards him, and the concern was evident in her eyes. 'She will not be happy about this, Oliver. You do know that, don't you?'

Oliver sighed. 'I am well aware of the fact, my dear. I also know that I do not have your complete agreement to the plan. But I cannot help but feel that the sooner Gillie is safely married to a man we can trust and respect, the less likely we are to suffer consequences that will make more than just Gillian unhappy.'

Helen was clearing out the small cupboard in her classroom when Gillian appeared in the doorway. She was holding a letter in her hand, and her face was as white as a ghost's.

'Miss de Coverdale, is this true? Is Oliver really going to marry me off to a man I do not even know?'

Helen sighed as she slowly got to her feet. It was the first time Gillian had spoken to her since the disastrous events of that fateful Sunday. Obviously, her concern over her guardian's plans was more than enough to make her forget her anger.

'I fear that is his intent, Gillian. He was very upset about what happened with Mr Wymington and he is anxious to see you happily settled.'

'But how can you say that? He is not concerned

with my happiness at all!' she cried, waving the letter in the air. 'He simply wishes me off his hands.'

'I do not believe that for a minute. Neither would you if you had seen how unhappy he was the last time I spoke with him.'

Gillian collapsed into a chair, her face a picture of despondency. 'Oh, it is all going so horribly wrong. First Oliver tells me I am to go back to Hertfordshire, and now I learn that I am to be married by Christmas. On top of that, I have been suffering agonies of guilt over having accused you of trying to lure Mr Wymington away. What must you think of me!'

'Gillian, there is no need—'

'There is every need,' the girl cried. 'How could I have accused you, my dearest friend, of behaving in such a manner? You, who have done nothing but show me kindness ever since I arrived. I am ashamed of myself for even thinking such a thing.' Gillian got up and flung herself into Helen's arms. 'Can you ever forgive me, my dear Miss de Coverdale?'

Nearly overcome with relief, Helen gave a shaky laugh. 'Dear child, of course I can forgive you. It was a very emotional day for all of us, and I think we all over-reacted a little. But now we must think of your future and what you are going to do about it.'

'I don't want to go back to Hertfordshire, Miss de Coverdale. I don't want to be married to someone I have never met. I would far rather stay here with you.'

Deciding for the moment not to tell Gillian that she wasn't going to be staying herself, Helen merely smiled and brushed the hair back from Gillian's face. 'Well, I cannot say for certain, my dear, but perhaps if you were to promise your guardian that you would not see Mr Wymington again—'

'Not see him! But—'

'Gillian, listen to me, it is the *only* way your guardian will allow you to stay. Understand that now, or know that you will have no choice but to return to Hertfordshire with him and do as he asks.'

Helen held her breath as Gillian slowly turned away. It was impossible to tell from the expression on her face what she was thinking. 'I doubt I shall ever find anyone as wonderful as Mr Wymington.'

'I know. But you will never know unless you try. Perhaps you will find someone even better.'

Gillian smiled, but Helen could tell her heart wasn't in it. She gave a half-hearted nod, and then turned and walked out of the room.

The entire episode left Helen feeling distinctly out of sorts. She could not bring herself to believe that Gillian would do something reckless in the short period of time she had left, but something about the look on the girl's face worried her excessively.

'Oh, Oliver, I do hope you're doing the right thing,' Helen whispered into the silence. 'And I do hope you get Gillian away from here before she has a chance to do something we will all live to regret!'

Oliver decided not to make the Guarding Academy his first stop upon his return to Northamptonshire. Instead, he headed for Abbot Quincey and the cottage reputed to belong to Mr Wymington's uncle. He assumed he would find Mr Wymington there. By all accounts he had not returned to his rooms in Hertfordshire, nor had he shown his face in London.

Which probably meant he was still in the area, waiting for an opportunity to see Gillian.

Well, he would find no success in that quarter, Oliver reflected grimly. Wymington would be told that if he didn't stay the hell away from her, he would be made to suffer the consequences. It was long past time someone put the man in his place. And if he refused, Oliver intended to demand satisfaction. After that, he planned to carry on to Guarding's and tell Mrs Guarding that he had rethought his decision with regard to Helen.

Oliver had wrestled long and hard with his conscience and in the end, had come to the conclusion that there was nothing to be gained by his forcing Helen to leave Mrs Guarding's employ. He hadn't changed his mind about removing Gillian from the school. And given that he and Sophie had already met with the younger Mr Riddleston and found him as delighted with the prospect of courting Gillian as they were of seeing it happen, there seemed to be no reason to exact further vengeance. It was enough that Gillian's life would be turned upside down, without doing the same to Helen's. She had already suffered enough. Oliver had no wish to be the cause of any further grief in her life.

Unfortunately, when Oliver arrived in Abbot Quincey and eventually located the cottage he was looking for, he was dismayed to find it securely locked, and seemingly in want of an owner.

'Are you looking for the old man who lived there, or the younger one?' a voice called to him from the street.

Oliver turned around and saw a middle-aged woman standing by the gate. She was plainly dressed and carried a baby on one ample hip. A little girl of about four clutched at the fabric of her skirt, while a blond-haired boy played in the dirt behind her.

'The younger one,' Oliver replied. 'I understood he was here visiting his uncle.'

'I don't know about that, sir,' the woman said. 'Gorse Cottage's been empty this six months or more. The old man died beginning of the year. Landlord found him when he came to collect the rent. Of course, nobody much bothered with him. They said he had relatives in London or somewhere about, but we never saw no visitors come.'

Oliver frowned. 'What about the young man who came here? When did you last see him?'

'Not for a week or so now, I shouldn't think. Hush Jane, I'll see to you shortly.' The woman sighed as she hiked the baby higher on her hip. 'Nice-looking young man, but definitely one for the ladies. I saw him come here with two of the girls from the village, and they all acting silly and giggling, as young girls will.'

Anger rose in Oliver's breast, but he struggled not to show it. 'I am grateful for your help, my good lady.' He walked back towards her and reaching into his pocket, pulled out a sovereign. 'Take this and buy something for you and your family.'

The woman looked at the gold coin in disbelief. 'A *sovereign*?' she whispered. 'You'd give so much to a stranger?'

Oliver smiled. 'What you just told me is worth that much.'

'Then I wish I could have told you more.' The woman winked at him as she tucked the coin in her pocket. 'I bid you thanks, sir, and a fine day to you.'

Oliver tipped his hat and watched her walk away. Then he turned to glance at the empty building behind him. So he had uncovered yet another of Wymington's lies. He wondered how many more there would be. For while it might well have been his uncle's cottage, it certainly wasn't to *visit* the old man that Wymington had come. Obviously he was using the cottage for his own purposes, not the least of which included a love nest—perhaps even one where he had hoped to lure Gillian.

A dangerous light glinted in Oliver's eyes. Yes, it was well he had set out on his course of action. Because he would find Sidney Wymington. And when he did, he would give him the thrashing he so richly deserved.

The only question was—where the hell was Wymington now?

'*Non credo di aver avuto il piacere,*' Helen said as she wrote the words on the chalkboard. 'Which means, I do not believe I have had the pleasure. Now, if you knew the person to whom you were being introduced, you would say—'

'*Credo che ci conosciamo,*' Oliver recited from the doorway.

As the girls began to giggle, Helen felt her cheeks grow warm. 'Mr Brandon!'

'Miss de Coverdale. Forgive my interrupting you in such a manner.'

Helen went to put the piece of chalk down—and promptly dropped it on the floor. 'That is quite all right.' She bent to pick it up, and stepped on the hem of her gown. 'We were just…finishing for the day.'

Blushing furiously, she smiled at her class. 'Thank you ladies. *A domani.*'

The girls offered a chorus of replies and then gathered up their books and filed out of the room. Oliver waited until the last of their footsteps had faded into silence before advancing further into the room. 'So, you have decided to leave Guarding's.'

Helen inclined her head. 'Mrs Guarding asked me to stay on until Christmas because we are still short-staffed. Otherwise I would already have gone.' She averted her gaze, wishing it wasn't so hard to see him like this. 'Have you come to…take Gillian home?'

'Yes. I would have been here earlier but I thought to pay a call on Mr Wymington. I went to the cottage where his uncle supposedly lived.'

Helen started. 'Supposedly?'

'A woman passing by told me that the man who owned the house died at least six months ago.'

'Six months!' Helen blanched. 'But…if that is the case, Mr Wymington must have intended—'

'Yes, I think we both know what Wymington intended,' Oliver interrupted darkly. 'He did have a key, so I can only assume it was his uncle's cottage, but he certainly did not come here to pay him any visits.'

'Mr Brandon, I hardly know what to say.'

'There's nothing to say, except to acknowledge that we were both correct in our assumptions about him. Which is why I think it best I take Gillian back to Hertfordshire as soon as possible. I cannot trust Wymington to keep his distance, and at the moment, I'm not sure I trust Gillian to keep hers either.' Oliver drew a deep breath. 'Nor am I convinced she would not agree to do something foolish if Wymington were to suggest it.'

Helen blanched. 'You think they might elope?'

'I cannot rule the possibility out. What I have learned of Wymington's character over the past few weeks has only served to deepen my dislike of him. He hasn't an honourable bone in his body, and for what it's worth, I am grateful to you for having confirmed my suspicions.'

'Is that why you came here now?' Helen asked.

'That, and to tell you that I intend to speak to Mrs Guarding about reinstating your position here.'

Helen gazed at him in confusion. *'What?'*

'There is no reason for you to leave the school, Miss de Coverdale,' Oliver said, his tone reflecting both warmth and concern for her. 'I was…angry when I spoke to Mrs Guarding. I was disappointed by what I perceived to be your betrayal. But I realise now that it wasn't a betrayal at all. You were simply doing what you thought best for Gillian. And in light of what you told me about your own past, how could I fault your motives? That is why I intend to speak to Mrs Guarding and assure her that I would be most pleased if you would return to your position here.' His mouth pulled into a thin-lipped smile. 'I only hope you will not think too badly of me for what has happened.'

'I could…never think badly of you, sir,' Helen said, painfully aware of the truth of the statement. 'I am just…surprised by the sudden turn of events. Are you going to see Gillian now?'

'I intend to speak to Mrs Guarding first. Then I shall see Gillian. Well, I suppose this really is good-bye, Miss de Coverdale.'

Not trusting her voice, Helen bent her head and curtseyed. There was so much she wanted to say to

him, and yet not a word of it was appropriate.
Likewise keeping his silence, Oliver merely bowed
from the waist, and then turned and left the room.

After he had gone, Helen slowly sank down at her
desk. She thought about everything he had told her,
including the forgiveness he wished her to have, and
then sadly closed her eyes. What was she to do? The
man she loved was walking out of her life.

And there was absolutely nothing she could do to
stop him.

As expected, Mrs Guarding was greatly relieved to
hear that Oliver no longer wished to see Miss de
Coverdale leave. His assurances that nothing would
be served by her resignation were warmly received,
as were his hopes that the slight breach of conduct
could be discreetly overlooked. The headmistress did
express her regrets that Gillian would be leaving
them, but she did not try to change Oliver's mind.
She merely thanked him for his leniency in allowing
Helen to stay, and then sent one of the girls to fetch
Gillian.

'She retired to her room with a megrim last night,'
Mrs Guarding informed him. 'I understand she has
stayed to her bed this morning with it as well.'

Oliver nodded his understanding. 'No doubt as a
result of my coming to take her home.'

Unfortunately, it was with considerable surprise
that they both learned a short while later that Gillian
was, in fact, not in her room.

'Perhaps she was feeling better and decided to
come downstairs, Mr Brandon,' the headmistress said.

'I believe she is scheduled for a class with Miss de Coverdale. I shall send a note and ask her to bring Gillian here.'

'That is quite all right,' Oliver said, already heading for the door. 'I shall go and fetch her myself.'

But Gillian was not in Helen's room, nor had Helen seen her that morning. And upon hearing as much, Oliver began to feel the first real stirrings of alarm.

'I think we should commence a search of the building,' he said, 'followed by a thorough check of the gardens and the—'

'Excuse me, Miss de Coverdale, Mr Brandon.'

Oliver broke off and turned to see Elizabeth Brookwell standing in the doorway. She was holding something in her hand and it was clear from the expression on her face that she was far from happy.

'What is it, Miss Brookwell?' Helen said quickly.

'I have a letter, Miss de Coverdale. For Mr Brandon.' The girl's voice was noticeably subdued. 'Gillian asked me to…give it to him when he arrived.'

'When did you last see Gillian?' Helen asked as Oliver went forward to take it.

'Very early this morning, Miss. She was dressed for going out, but when I asked her where she was going, she wouldn't tell me. She just gave me this letter and said I was to make sure Mr Brandon received it.' Elizabeth's bottom lip quivered. 'She said I wasn't to give it to him until this evening, but I thought it best not to wait that long.'

'Thank you, Miss Brookwell, you may go.'

As the girl silently departed, Oliver broke the seal and read the letter aloud.

Dear Oliver:

I am sorry to disappoint you, but I have left
with Mr Wymington. I know you do not approve
of him, but I love him, and I could not bear the
thought of being forced into marriage with someone else—especially someone I do not even
know. Please do not worry about me. Mr
Wymington loves me and has promised to take
good care of me. He assures me this is the only
way we can be together. I shall write again once
we are husband and wife.

'Love, Gillian,' Oliver finished on a whisper.

Helen felt as though the room was spinning all
around her. 'Dear God, we must stop them!'

'We must indeed, but how much of a head start
have they?'

Thankfully, a visit to the stables provided them
with the answers they needed. One of the lads had
chanced to see a closed carriage drawn by a single
horse pull up to the back door of the school around
five o'clock that morning, and minutes later, a young
lady dressed in a travelling cloak and carrying a small
case emerge from the school and climb up beside the
gentleman.

It seemed that Mr Wymington had indeed, persuaded Gillian to elope with him.

Helen began to tremble. 'They will head for
Scotland.'

Oliver nodded. 'Without question. Which is why I
must set off immediately.' His expression was bleak.
'Wymington has only one horse, but the gig is light
and they have the advantage of a considerable head
start.'

'Poor foolish girl,' Helen whispered. 'She has no idea what she is doing.'

'Of course not. To her, it will all be some great adventure. I only hope to God I can catch them before it is too late.'

'Let me come with you, Mr Brandon,' Helen cried suddenly. 'I can't help but feel that I am partially to blame for what has happened.'

'This isn't your fault, Miss de Coverdale, but I would be grateful for your company. It is imperative that we find them!'

Helen did not voice her unspoken thoughts as she hurried towards his waiting carriage. They had to find the miscreant pair indeed. All they could do was hope that it wasn't already too late.

Chapter Thirteen

Drawn by a pair of fleet-footed blacks, Oliver's carriage made excellent time along the dusty road. Assuming that Wymington would head for Gretna, they set out on an identical path and drew comfort from the fact that they could travel the road faster with two horses than Wymington could with one. But Wymington had the advantage of time, and in a race like this, every second counted!

Helen said very little on the frenzied drive north. She was too wrapped up in her own thoughts to offer aimless conversation. Oliver too was restrained, fixing his concentration on the team and on maintaining a steady pace.

'They cannot be so very far ahead of us,' he said, his eyes scanning the horizon. 'Thank God they set off this morning and not last night. Otherwise we would be too late to save her, even now.'

Helen knew all too well what Oliver was referring to. Had Gillian been forced to spend even one night at an inn with Mr Wymington, her reputation would have been irrevocably lost. The best they could have hoped for then was marriage.

They passed through a number of small villages as they headed for the border. Oliver stopped at one coaching inn to enquire about the passage of a gig carrying a young lady and a gentleman, and described them as best he could. Most fortuitously, he was given the very good news that yes, a young couple matching their description had stopped there a little while earlier, but that they had carried on after only a brief delay. And no, they had not gone in for a meal or anything else, as far as the man could remember. Oliver had nodded his satisfaction, and then urged the horses on.

Finally, a few hours later, Helen gasped as she spotted a small carriage drawn by a single horse away in the distance ahead of them. 'Look, Mr Brandon, there!'

'Yes, I see them.' Oliver flicked the whip over his horses' heads with renewed vigour. 'It would seem we are to be spared a considerable amount of grief. Tell me, Miss de Coverdale. Would you be able to drive this carriage if forced by circumstances to do so?'

Surprised, Helen glanced at him. 'Yes, I am sure I could.'

'Good. There was a decent-looking inn in the last village we passed. Perhaps you would take Gillian back there and wait for me while I deal with Mr Wymington.'

'Yes, of course.'

'Good. Now, I suggest you hold on. I am going to try to overtake them.'

It was a daring move. The road was considerably narrower here than it had been in other places, and Helen gasped as Oliver closed the distance and then urged his carriage alongside Mr Wymington's, causing them both to sway and bounce precariously. She forgot her nervousness, however, when she saw Gillian's white face staring back at her.

'Draw to a halt, sir!' Oliver shouted. 'You can go no farther!'

Wymington turned to glare at them, an ugly expression marring the handsome lines of his face. For a moment, Helen wondered if he would ignore Oliver's order and push on regardless. But he must have seen something in Oliver's face that convinced him of the futility of continued flight. Reluctantly, he drew the lathered bay to a halt.

Oliver sprang down and ignoring Wymington, went immediately to see to Gillian. 'Are you all right?' he asked as she shakily emerged from the carriage.

Gillian's eyes were the size of saucers. 'Of course, but…what are you doing here?'

'I have come to take you home. Surely you did not think I would allow this abomination to take place!'

'But I love him!' she cried desperately.

'I will hear no more of this, Gillian,' Oliver snapped. 'Go with Miss de Coverdale. She will see you safely back.'

'Why? What are you going to do?'

'I am going to have a word with Mr Wymington.'

Impulsively, Gillian reached for his arm. 'He did not force me to come, Oliver. Please, you must believe me. I am here of my own free will!'

'Yes, no doubt after he convinced you of how wonderful your life together would be.' Oliver glanced at Helen and she saw the anger shimmering in his eyes. 'Take her back to the inn and wait for me.'

Helen nodded, and moved towards Gillian. 'Come, my dear. We must leave here.'

'Oliver, please don't hurt him!' Gillian cried.

'Do as I say, Gillian!'

Sobbing, Gillian put her hand to her mouth. She ran back to Oliver's carriage and flung herself into the seat.

'Take me away from here,' she cried as Helen climbed up beside her.

Suppressing a sigh, Helen gathered up the reins and set the pair to a brisk trot. Gillian obviously had no desire to stay and listen to what Oliver had to say to her beloved Mr Wymington.

Gillian was very quiet on the ride back to the Rose and Crown, and wisely, Helen did not press her for conversation. A great deal had happened over the past twelve hours and she had no doubt that Gillian was trying to make sense of it all. Only a short time ago, she had been headed for Scotland with the man she planned to marry. Now, she was driving back to an inn with a former teacher at her side, after having left her dashing young man at the side of the road to face a very angry and displeased guardian. Indeed, there was much for her to think about.

Helen, however, was not sorry for the silence. It gave her ample opportunity to focus her attention on her driving. While she was relieved that the blacks had such responsive mouths, they were spirited creatures demanding of her full attention. She did not wish to put them at a hole and risk possible injury to the animals or to themselves.

Fortunately, it wasn't long before she got the feel of the reins back and was able to relax a little. But she could not relax her mind, filled as it was with the enormity of everything that had happened. What would Oliver do now? What was he saying to poor Mr Wymington? Helen knew she was probably foolish to feel any kind of pity for the man, but she would not have wished to be in his place. Oliver's anger would be frightful, and while she knew that duels were seldom fought in England any more, this would be a matter of honour. Helen was quite sure that, given the type of man Oliver was, he would demand justice.

At the Rose and Crown, Helen asked the landlord for a room where they might rest awhile and then ordered a light meal for Gillian. The poor child had not eaten anything, given that Mr Wymington had been anxious to reach his destination. Helen had no stomach for food, and ordered nothing for herself. Instead, she sat next to Gillian at the table and tried to break through the girl's wall of silence.

'Did you really think about what you were doing?' Helen asked gently. 'Your brother was nearly beside himself with worry.'

Tears bubbled in Gillian's eyes. 'Sidney told me he loved me. He said he…wanted to marry me.' She looked up at Helen and her mouth began to quiver. 'He even showed me the ring he had bought.'

As Gillian began to weep in earnest, Helen pulled her into her arms and held her close. Poor child. How hard it must all seem to her. Indeed, Helen remembered all too well the pain and the grief she had suffered in the days following her separation from Thomas. At times, she had wondered if she would ever stop crying.

'I know this seems like the end of the world,

Gillie,' Helen whispered against her hair, 'but you must believe it is for the best. Mr Wymington was dashing and handsome, but he was not an honourable man. I know that is hard for you to accept, but I am telling you the truth, dearest. He would have taken advantage of you.'

'He t-told me you would t-try to turn me against him,' Gillian blubbered. 'He told me you would t-try to make me...think ill of him.'

'Yes, because Mr Wymington is a very smart man.' Helen brushed the blonde hair back from Gillian's forehead. 'Men like him always know what to say to impressionable young women. He knew how to make you believe everything he said.'

Gillian sniffed. 'I hate Oliver for doing this. I *hate* him!'

'Hush, child,' Helen crooned, rocking her close. 'You mustn't say things like that because I know you do not mean them. Oliver did what he did because he loves you. He was very worried about you.'

'But there was no need. We were going to be married.' Gillian's face crumpled into tears again. 'He bought me a ring...'

Helen knew there was nothing she could say to make the pain go away, so she just let the girl cry. Time would heal the raw edges, but for now, the wound was too fresh, the pain too deep. Gillian would suffer much before she came to terms with the reality of Mr Wymington's deceit, and for a while, it would be difficult for all of them. Helen only hoped Oliver would have the patience and the understanding to deal with it.

Oliver joined them at the inn a short while later. Helen met him at the door of the small, cosy parlour and knew without having to ask that it had been a difficult interview. His eyes were dark, his lips pressed together in a tight, angry line. But he said not a word about Mr Wymington, asking only after Gillian's welfare, and her own.

'I am fine, sir, and thankfully, Gillian is asleep,' Helen assured him as she closed the door. 'She had been crying ever since we arrived.'

'Thank you for bringing her back here, Miss de Coverdale, and for taking care of her.'

'There is no need to thank me, sir; I would have done it without your asking. But…where is…Mr Wymington?'

'On his way to London.' Oliver's face closed down. 'We shall not be hearing from him again.'

Helen's eyes opened wide. 'Did you threaten him?'

'Not in so many words. I gave him the choice of settling the matter with pistols at dawn, or by writing a letter of confession to Gillian in which he told her the truth of his intentions.' Oliver withdrew a letter from his pocket. 'Needless to say, he chose the latter. I assured him he had made the right decision, since at least this way he was able to escape with his life.'

Helen looked at the letter but did not ask to read it. 'What will he do now?'

'Take the money I gave him and use it to buy his commission.'

'You *gave* him money?'

'I wanted to make sure he had enough to go on his way. But I assured him that if he ever tried to contact Gillian again, I would kill him.'

Helen shuddered. She had no doubt Oliver meant it. There was something in his tone that convinced her it was not an idle threat. Mr Wymington had made the mistake of trifling with someone Oliver loved. If he valued his life, he would not make that mistake again.

Within the hour, they set off for Steep Abbot. Gillian was very quiet getting into the carriage. Her eyes were red-rimmed and swollen, and Helen knew it was because Oliver had shown her the letter. The poor child had clutched it almost pathetically to her breast, the look of hurt and confusion on her face heartbreaking to see. Clearly, the truth of Wymington's defection had come as a crushing disappointment.

It was well after dark by the time they reached the school. Helen took Gillian up to her room and spent a few minutes with her there before returning downstairs. Then, together, she and Oliver went to see Mrs Guarding.

Not surprisingly, the headmistress was in a rare state of agitation.

'Helen, Mr Brandon, I am so relieved that you have returned.' Mrs Guarding glanced from one to the other with a look of deep apprehension. 'Is everything all right?'

'Everything is fine,' Oliver assured her. 'Thankfully, we were able to intercept Gillian and Mr Wymington in time to stop them from marrying. Or from anything worse happening.'

The headmistress sagged noticeably against her desk. 'Thank God for that. Where is Mr Wymington?'

'The gentleman will not be troubling us again,' Oliver said quietly. 'He is even now on his way to London to secure a new position with the militia.'

'And Gillian? How is the poor child?'

Oliver sighed. 'Disappointed. Broken-hearted. Mr Wymington wrote out a confession admitting to his true motives in courting her. Needless to say, when Gillian read it, she was devastated. She'd believed all along that we had conspired to make Wymington sound like a fraud. It shook her to learn that we had been telling her the truth.'

'Poor child.' Mrs Guarding's kindly face was filled with compassion. 'How terribly confused and betrayed she must be feeling right now. It is never easy to recover from disappointments of the heart. But she is young and time will heal the wounds she has suffered today. Eventually, she will be as bright and happy as ever.'

'Yes, but I think it is still best I take her back to Hertfordshire with me,' Oliver said. 'I will feel better knowing that she is close during these next few weeks. I know she doesn't like me very much right now, but I want her to know that I care about her regardless.'

Mrs Guarding sighed. 'Yes, I think it is important that she does know that, Mr Brandon. Well, I shall make arrangements to have her cases brought down. When do you wish to leave?'

'I think the sooner the better. With luck she will sleep in the carriage.'

Helen listened to the conversation in silence. She refused to allow herself to dwell on what it meant, because she knew that if she did, she would be every bit as heart-broken as Gillian. Oliver was taking his ward back to Hertfordshire. Which meant that he would have no reason to return to Steep Abbot.

Ever.

* * *

The pattern of Helen's days soon fell back into their former routine. It was a rhythm that had been established long before Oliver Brandon had come into her life—and her heart. The girls had all been sorry to see Gillian go, of course, but Helen knew their grief would pass and that life would go on for all of them. Such was the way of the world. But it was hard to pretend that everything was all right in *her* world. Helen felt as though her heart had been torn asunder, and that her life had become a sad and empty vacuum; a vacuum where love should have existed.

Mrs Guarding continued to be supportive. She gave Helen extra time away from school, and surprisingly, Helen found herself eager to take advantage of it. She was finding it increasingly difficult to concentrate on her studies. She could not muster the same level of enthusiasm for her classes. Instead, she took to wandering through the woods near Steep Abbot, enjoying the freshness of the crisp autumn air and savouring the peace and quiet to be found in the shelter of the huge old trees. Somehow, she took comfort in the familiarity of nature.

On a beautiful clear day near the end of October, Helen wandered down to the pond where Desirée had first met her dashing Lord Buckworth. She had never ventured this far into the Steep Wood before, and for a moment, she just stood in silent admiration of the beauty all around her. No wonder Desirée had come here so often. There was a kind of serenity about the place. A feeling of peace. It was almost as though the problems of the outside world had no place within these leafy bowers.

She sat by the grassy edge of the river and threw

stones into the water, watching the ripples fan out in ever-increasing circles. As she did, Helen tried not to think about Oliver. She tried not to remember the sound of his voice, or the breathless way he'd made her feel every time he spoke to her. Because to remember those things only brought it all back.

Funny. He had never even spoken her name, and yet Helen knew how sweet it would sound upon his lips. She often whispered his own name aloud, lingering over it, wondering if he would smile at hearing her say it. He never would, of course, because there would never be anything between them to allow such familiarities. He would always be Mr Brandon to her, and she Miss de Coverdale to him. A wealthy gentleman, especially one with connections to the aristocracy, would never contemplate marriage to a lowly schoolmistress.

Helen sighed as she watched a single leaf drop from an overhead branch and land on the glassy surface of the water. Oh yes, he was well-connected. Gillian had told her as much during one of their last conversations. She had informed her that his aunt was Viscountess Endersley, an imperious lady who lived with her husband on a magnificent estate in Kent. Apparently, Lady Endersley travelled north at least six times a year to visit her family, and it was widely known that Oliver was her favourite. She had, over the last little while, presented several young women to him in the hopes he might find one amongst them who would be suitable to becoming his wife, and she had been *most* disappointed when he had declined them all.

Helen's lips curved in a wistful smile. She could only imagine what Lady Endersley would say if

Oliver were to express interest in a schoolmistress. She would never condone such a *mésalliance*. For Oliver to marry so far beneath him would be unthinkable.

Still, all of that meant nothing in the overall scheme of things, because Oliver had not *expressed* any interest in her. Oh, he had been charming in her company, and even flattering upon occasion. But there had been nothing in his conduct to convince her that he held her in any particular esteem. She had enjoyed the brief time they had spent together, but he had not misled her in any way, nor allowed her to believe there was anything between them. She was his ward's teacher. He was her pupil's guardian.

There was really nothing more to it than that.

It was the middle of November before Helen heard from Gillian again. The letter arrived innocently enough with the midday post, but as Helen read it over in the privacy of her room after classes that night, her eyes began to widen in a mixture of shock, fascination and bewilderment at the unexpected news.

My dear Miss de Coverdale

You will no doubt be surprised at receiving this, but I simply had to write and tell you. I am in love with a wonderful young man and engaged to be married! Yes, I know you will be shocked, but it has all happened so quickly I can scarce believe it myself. My betrothal celebration is to take place on the nineteenth, and I am writing to ask if you will attend. Oliver has already secured Mrs Guarding's approval for the visit, and if you are agreeable, he will send a carriage to bring you to Shefferton Hall on Wednesday next, where you are to remain with us until Saturday.

I do hope you will agree to make the journey. I have missed you terribly, and hope you are as eager to see me as I am to see you. I have so much to tell you! Oliver too, is anxious to renew his acquaintance.

Your dear friend
Gillian Gresham

Helen let the letter fall to her lap and then stared at the wall in disbelief. Gillian was *in love*? But how in the world had such a thing come to pass—and so quickly? The child had barely been back in Hertfordshire a month. How could she have met someone and fallen in love with him in such a short period of time? More importantly, was this the arranged marriage Oliver had spoken of?

Helen picked up the letter and read it over again:

…Oliver has already secured Mrs Guarding's approval for the visit, and if you are agreeable, he will send a carriage to bring you here to Shefferton Hall on Wednesday next, where you are to remain with us until Saturday.

Goodness, Oliver certainly wasn't leaving anything to chance, Helen reflected. He had gone to Mrs Guarding and gained her approval for the visit before Helen had even been made aware of it. He was even sending a carriage so that transportation might not be an issue. '…Oliver too, is anxious to renew his acquaintance.' Helen decided not to read too much into that. While she wished with all her heart that the sentiment might be a genuine one, she knew better than to allow herself the luxury of believing it. Gillian was the one who wished her to be present at the betrothal celebration, so it was only natural that it was she who would have persuaded Oliver to invite her. And relieved that Mr Wymington was no longer the object of her affection, Oliver had probably been willing to do anything to make Gillian happy, even to allow her dear Miss de Coverdale to be present at the celebration.

Still, it was flattering to know that Gillian cared enough to invite her *and* that Oliver had no serious objections to her being there. And surely if the Brandons saw nothing wrong with a schoolmistress mingling with polite society, neither should she.

Chapter Fourteen

November, 1812

Shefferton Hall was a fine old house, built before the time of Elizabeth I and mellowed even further by the relentless passage of time. It slumbered against the natural beauty of gently sloping hills and wide-open meadows bordered by dense hedgerows and the occasional low stone wall. The gravelled drive was long and lined on either side with tall trees, the branches of which joined together to form a canopy of green overhead. It cut through a fine timber bush and then curved towards the Hall, finally allowing Helen her first glimpse of the majestic house, and causing her to catch her breath in wonder.

She had expected a lovely property. She had not expected anything like this.

A sudden movement drew Helen's attention towards the impressive front entrance. Gillian was standing on the top step, dancing up and down and waving her hands. Helen smiled and waved back, trying not to admit to the excitement she was already beginning to feel.

It was hard to believe that she was actually here in Hertfordshire. That she had been invited to stay at this magnificent home by the family of one of her former pupils. Harder still to believe that within moments she would be face to face with Oliver again. How would she feel upon seeing him? Helen wondered as the carriage finally drew to a halt and a liveried footman let down the stairs. What would she say to him, and how would he respond? More importantly, would she be able to keep the depth of her feelings from him for the several days she would be called upon to be in his company?

'Miss de Coverdale!' Gillian cried as she ran forward. 'How splendid to see you again! I am so very pleased you have come.'

'And I am very pleased to have been invited,' Helen said, returning the girl's affectionate embrace. 'But I must say the news came as something of a shock.'

'Yes, I knew it would.' Gillian laughed as though it were all a wonderful joke. 'Oliver said you would be astonished. But we can talk of that later. Right now you must come and meet Sophie.' Gillian linked her arm through Helen's and turned to lead the way back inside. 'I have told her all about you and she is most anxious to make your acquaintance.'

The trepidation Helen felt at the thought of meeting Gillian's stepsister vanished within moments of their being introduced. Mrs Sophie Llewellyn was every bit as delightful as Gillian had led her to believe. Striking in appearance, she was very tall and slender, and was possessed of the warmest, most gracious

smile Helen had ever seen. She immediately set about
to making her feel at ease, and as the conversation
flowed between them, Helen couldn't help but like
the elegant lady whose bright green eyes seemed to
contain a perpetual twinkle.

'I am so glad you agreed to come, Miss de
Coverdale,' Sophie said when they were all comfortably seated in the beautifully appointed drawing-
room. 'We have heard a great deal about you since
Gillian returned from Steep Abbot, and I must say, it
has all been of a most flattering nature.'

Helen felt the warmth rise to her cheeks, uncomfortable at being the centre of attention. 'I cannot
imagine what Miss Gresham could have said to elicit
such praise, Mrs Llewellyn, but I can assure you that
I enjoyed having her as one of my pupils. She is a
gifted watercolourist and did a credible job with her
Italian. I am very pleased at having been invited to
celebrate this wonderful occasion with her.'

'Good afternoon, Miss de Coverdale.'

The voice that fell so sweetly on her ears caused
Helen to jump and her heart to turn over in her breast.
Oliver. She turned slowly and saw him standing in
the doorway. His dark hair was windblown and his
cheeks were ruddy from the cold. He looked to have
just returned from a ride, and it seemed to Helen that
he was even more dashing than he had been upon the
occasion of their last meeting.

Surely it was not possible for a man to grow so
very much more handsome in the space of only a few
short weeks?

'You smile at my greeting,' Oliver observed as he
walked into the room. 'Was it something in my choice
of words?'

'Forgive me, Mr Brandon. My amusement had nothing to do with what you said or with anything about you,' Helen hastened to say. 'I was merely thinking about something Gillian said to me a few weeks back.' She cleared her throat and wished that her quickened pulse would settle so that the annoyingly breathless quality of her voice would also disappear. 'Thank you for all the trouble you have gone to on my behalf. Both in speaking to Mrs Guarding and to arranging transportation for bringing me here.'

Oliver tipped his head. 'Neither was in any way troublesome. Mrs Guarding informed me that you had forgone the pleasure of a trip to London to see your good friend married, so she was more than happy to allow you this little outing in its place. And while I admit that Gillian's betrothal ball will hardly replicate the pomp and ceremony of a full-blown society wedding, I daresay we shall acquit ourselves reasonably well.'

'Dearest Oliver, you are being far too modest,' Gillian piped up. 'Considering all the arrangements you and Sophie have made, I am quite sure my betrothal ball will be the most elegant to be seen in Hertfordshire this year, and that my wedding will be the equal of any to be held in London. You will come to my wedding, won't you, Miss de Coverdale?' Gillian said, turning impulsively towards Helen. 'I cannot imagine getting married without you being there. In fact, perhaps you would like to—'

'Before you start making too many plans for Miss de Coverdale,' Sophie interrupted, 'perhaps I should show her to her room. I am sure she would like to rest before dinner. Travelling is such a tiresome occupation, is it not, Miss de Coverdale?'

'It is indeed, Mrs Llewellyn,' Helen said, smiling her gratitude. 'Thank you.'

'Oh, very well,' Gillian grumbled, clearly put out at having her friend whisked away so quickly. 'But we shall continue this over dinner. And then you must tell me what is happening at Guarding's, and how many of the girls miss me and ask after me.'

'Impertinent minx,' Oliver drawled affectionately. 'I doubt any of them have spared you so much as a thought since you left.'

'Oliver!'

'Pay him no mind, Gillian,' Sophie said, rising. 'You know how he likes to tease you. I am quite sure *all* the young ladies at Guarding's are anxious to hear how you go on, and to know all about your upcoming nuptials.'

'They are indeed, Mrs Llewellyn. In fact,' Helen said, wishing to set Gillian's mind at rest, 'you will be pleased to learn that I have brought letters from several of the girls who are anxious for news of her.'

Gillian's face brightened. 'Really? They have truly taken the time to write?'

'They have. I shall bring the letters down to dinner. Unless you would consider the timing inappropriate?' Helen said, glancing uncertainly at her hostess.

'It will not be inappropriate, Miss de Coverdale. Most of our guests will be arriving tomorrow, so I thought it might be pleasant to have a quiet, informal dinner this evening. It will give us an opportunity to become better acquainted with you.'

Grateful that she would be spared the rigours of a formal dinner, Helen inclined her head. 'There is little enough to know, Mrs Llewellyn. My life has been very quiet compared to most.'

'Well, I am sure we shall find something to talk about.'

'And we seldom find ourselves at a loss for conversation with Gillian about,' Oliver added. 'Even if we cannot vouch for the significance of its content.'

'Oh, now that is not fair, Oliver!' Gillian cried. '*You* have told me that I am a skilled conversationalist and that I find far more interesting subjects to talk about than most of my friends!'

'Come, Miss de Coverdale,' Sophie whispered. 'I shall take you upstairs and see you settled.' She drew Helen to her feet as Oliver and Gillian continued their good-natured bickering. 'Once these two get started on a discussion, there is no telling when it will end!'

The room Helen had been given for the duration of her visit was as pretty as she could have wished. It was bright and spacious, with mullioned windows that gave view towards the south-west, and walls that were papered in a soft lemon-coloured silk. The bedspread and curtains were of a slightly deeper hue, while the tapestry seat-covers and bed pillows all contained traces of the same warm shade. 'Oh, how lovely!' Helen exclaimed upon entering.

'Yes, it is nice, isn't it.' Sophie agreed. 'It was originally Catherine's room. Gillian's mother,' she explained at seeing Helen's look of confusion. 'She moved in here after my father died. Catherine loved yellow. She said it reminded her of daffodils and sunshine, and that she liked to have it around her as much as possible. Which was not in the least surprising.' Sophie glanced around the room and her lips curved in a smile of affection. 'If there was ever a woman blessed with a sunny disposition, it was Catherine Gresham.'

Helen nodded as she moved towards the elegant, four-poster bed and gazed around the room. It *was* exceedingly bright and sunny, and it certainly did make one feel cheerful. Unfortunately, one of the maids had already unpacked what few belongings Helen had brought with her out upon the bed and the comparison between her drab, dark school gowns and the sumptuous colours everywhere else was striking in the extreme.

'Well, I shall leave you alone to rest, Miss de Coverdale,' Sophie said, seeming not to notice. 'If you are in need of assistance, you have only to ring the bell for Trudy. She is a most accommodating young woman and will make sure you have everything you need.'

'Thank you, Mrs Llewellyn. I am sure I shall be very comfortable.'

'Good.' Sophie smiled then, and hesitated. 'By the by, I fear you may not have had time to prepare a new gown for Gillian's betrothal party. Indeed, you were scarce given time to ready yourself, let alone to acquire new clothes. But you need not concern yourself about such matters.' She walked towards the large wardrobe in the corner of the room and opened the doors. 'Perhaps you will be able to find something in here to your liking.'

The doors swung open and Helen gasped at the startling array of clothes that suddenly came into view. There were silk and satin evening gowns, elegant walking gowns and stylish riding habits, along with a veritable abundance of bonnets, boots, gloves, and shawls. Everything the well-dressed lady could possibly need.

'Gracious! Who do all of these clothes belong to?'

'Most of them were Catherine's,' Sophie told her. 'She absolutely adored clothes. She would sit for hours pouring over copies of *La Belle Assemblee* or *Ackermann's*. And she was most particular when it came to having new things. She would not wear anything that was not of the first stare.' Sophie drew out a lovely gown in a warm shade of apricot silk and held it up for Helen's inspection. 'As you can see, the styling is somewhat out of date, but the fabric is excellent and the beadwork quite lovely.' She cast Helen a sideways glance. 'Are you at all skilled with a needle, Miss de Coverdale?'

Helen nodded, already assessing the degree of difficulty involved in altering the lovely garment. 'Yes, I am.'

'Good. Then I think this gown—or any of the others—could easily be made wearable. Catherine was not unlike you in size.' She offered Helen an apologetic glance as she laid the gown on the bed. 'I would offer to lend you one of my own, but I fear the work entailed in altering it would be far more extensive than what you will encounter here.'

Helen bit back a smile. While the length of Mrs Llewellyn's gowns would not pose a problem, the width across the bodice—or the lack thereof—certainly would.

'You are exceedingly kind, Mrs Llewellyn,' Helen said quietly, 'and I am more grateful to you than I can say. I am sure I shall be able to find something in the wardrobe that I can alter in time for tomorrow night's festivities.'

'And for dinner this evening, if you like.' Sophie held up the apricot silk again. 'With your dark hair, this shade becomes you very well, and I do not think there would be more than an hour or two's work to make it suitable.'

Helen bit her lip, wanting to take advantage of the lady's generous offer, but not at all sure she should. 'Will Gillian not mind me wearing her mother's clothes?' she asked. 'She might feel that I have…intruded on Catherine's memory in some way.'

'Gillian will be *delighted* to see you wearing them,' Sophie assured her. 'She has often remarked to me that it is a pity someone cannot make use of them, being that they are so very lovely. And I am quite sure Oliver will be happy to see you so attired.'

Helen hastily turned away, not wishing the other woman to catch sight of her burning cheeks. 'There is no reason why he should be, Mrs Llewellyn. Mr Brandon has been polite to me on the few occasions we have been in each other's company, but there is nothing to our acquaintance beyond that.'

'Perhaps, but my brother has made mention of you several times, Miss de Coverdale, and it is not like Oliver to speak of ladies with whom he has had so brief an acquaintance.'

'Well, I am sure he has only done so because I grew close to Gillian during the time she was at Mrs Guarding's Academy,' Helen replied. Then, desperately needing to change the subject, she smiled and said, 'I hope you will forgive me for asking, but what is the name of the gentleman Gillian has become betrothed to?'

'Good Lord. You mean Gillian didn't tell you in her letter?'

'No. She only said it had all happened very quickly, and that she could hardly believe it herself.'

'Well, yes, I think it caught us all a little off guard,' Sophie admitted with a chuckle, 'though not unpleasantly so since Oliver did ask me to arrange it. The gentleman's name is Nigel Riddleston. He is the eldest son of Sir John and Lady Riddleston of Kestwick Park in Wiltshire. My husband, whom you will meet at dinner this evening, knows the family very well and it was actually he who arranged their first meeting in London last year. Unfortunately, there did not appear to be any interest on Gillian's part, and not long after that, she met Mr Wymington. Strangely enough, however, this last time Gillian saw Mr Riddleston, everything was quite different.' Sophie smiled as she turned and walked towards the bedroom door. 'I think it safe to say that for Gillian, it was definitely a case of love at second sight!'

Helen spent considerable time debating whether or not to wear the elegant silk gown to dinner that night. Despite Mrs Llewellyn's assurances that no one would mind, she couldn't help but feel that she was intruding somehow; that she had no right to take Catherine Gresham's clothes and alter them to suit herself. But then, after further consideration, Helen decided that she was probably just being foolish. She had no wish to embarrass Gillian in front of her family and friends, and that was precisely what she would do if she were to appear wearing one of her dreary school gowns. Surely it would not be so very wrong to make use of one or two of the gowns hanging in the wardrobe. Certainly Mrs Llewellyn did not seem to think so.

In the end, Helen was exceedingly glad she did decide to wear the apricot silk because the meal was neither the casual affair it was supposed to be, nor the intimate family gathering Mrs Llewellyn had planned. The unexpected arrival of the Viscount and Viscountess Endersley and their two sons—one newly married, the other accompanied by his noticeably increasing wife—along with all of their attendant maids, valets and assorted underlings shortly before five o'clock threw the carefully laid plans asunder and the entire household into disarray.

Fortunately, the ever-efficient Sophie soon had matters under control. She saw to it that the new arrivals were warmly greeted and settled in their rooms and then informed the butler that he should prepare the formal dining-room for the evening meal, rather than the common parlour where they had planned to eat. Lastly, she went to the kitchens herself to advise Mrs White of the last-minute guests, and to personally apologise for the extra work involved in their arrival.

Helen was both relieved and dismayed by the advent of Oliver's toplofty relations. Relieved because it meant she would not be singled out for attention over dinner, but dismayed because she knew it would be inappropriate for her to attend. She might well be an invited guest to Gillian's ball, but she doubted the Viscount and his wife would appreciate sharing dinner conversation with a schoolmistress from Steep Abbot. And with that in mind, she hastily sent a note to Mrs Llewellyn advising her that she would not come down for dinner, but that she would take a tray in her room.

Unfortunately, not long after despatching Trudy with the message, Helen was herself summoned to the drawing-room. To her surprise, it was not Mrs Llewellyn who awaited her there, but Oliver.

'Oh! Mr Brandon.'

He turned at the sound of her surprised exclamation and offered her a tentative smile. 'I take it you were not expecting to see me, Miss de Coverdale?'

'No indeed, sir, I was not.' Helen felt the warmth steel into her cheeks again. 'I asked Trudy to extend my regrets to Mrs Llewellyn.'

'Which she did. But since I happened to be with my sister at the time the message was delivered, I volunteered to speak to you myself, since we were both in agreement as to the response.'

Helen bit her lip. 'I was not expecting a response.'

'Not even to be told that we would both very much like you to join us for dinner this evening?'

The sentiment was a generous one, but it was not what Helen had been hoping to hear. 'I do not think it would be appropriate, Mr Brandon. You have guests to attend to now.'

His mouth lifted a fraction. 'Are you not a guest?'

'Well, yes, but these are family members who I am quite sure would not appreciate the presence of a schoolmistress at their table.'

Oliver lifted one dark eyebrow in surprise. 'Are you forgetting that this is *my* house, Miss de Coverdale? And that I am the one who decides who sits down to my table?'

'I have not forgotten at all. Nevertheless, I am inclined to believe that your aunt and uncle's position in society—'

'My uncle is a jovial fellow,' Oliver interrupted smoothly. 'He drinks, perhaps a touch more than he ought, but he is happy enough when in his cups. And I have never heard him speak a harsh word to anyone, no matter what their position in life.'

Helen moved slowly towards the fireplace. 'Your uncle sounds like a most amiable gentleman.'

'Amiable indeed. As are his two sons.' Oliver stopped to run his fingers over a fine porcelain vase. 'Mr Richard Endersley, the eldest, has been married for two years. His wife is the middle daughter of Sir Geoffrey Netherby, late of Portsmouth. It was considered a good match, and my aunt was pleased. Mr Peter Endersley, my aunt's younger son, is only recently married and is anticipating the birth of his first child in the spring. His wife is the youngest daughter of a clergyman.'

Helen blinked her surprise. 'A clergyman?'

'A clergyman. From the North Country.'

'Really.' Helen felt a smile tugging at the corners of her mouth. 'And was your aunt as pleased with her younger son's choice of a wife as she was with her eldest's?'

'Not at first, but she has come to love Sarah as dearly as though she were a duchess.' Oliver's smile flashed. 'So you see, Miss de Coverdale, there is no reason for *you* to feel that your presence at the table this evening would be in any way lacking simply because you are a schoolmistress. Was your own father not a barrister?'

'Well, yes, but—'

'Then we need say no more. Except that I will be sorely disappointed if I do not see your lovely face gracing my table this evening.'

The unexpected compliment brought Helen's arguments to a halt—and the blood rushing to her cheeks.

'Of course, I realise it may not only be the early arrival of my aunt and uncle which has caused you this concern,' Oliver continued, his voice dropping. 'It may be that you are only using it as an excuse to avoid someone else's company at dinner this evening.'

Helen inhaled sharply. Surely he did not think she was desirous of avoiding *his* company, simply because of what had happened with Gillian?

'I cannot think what you mean, sir. I would certainly have no reason for avoiding the company of…anyone else who might be at your table this evening.'

'I am relieved to hear it. Because I should not like to think I have offended you in any way.' Oliver took a step closer to her, and rested his fingers lightly upon her arm. 'That would disturb me even more than would your absence from my table this evening.'

His sudden proximity was alarming in the extreme and Helen prayed he would not be able to see how rapidly her heart was beating. 'You need have no cause for concern, sir, for you have not offended me in any way. Indeed, you have been…all that is gracious. Now if you will excuse me, I think I should be…returning to my room.'

'Then you will be joining me…us…for dinner this evening?'

Helen closed her eyes. When he asked her in such a manner, how could she deny him? 'Yes, of course,' she whispered. Then, because she could think of nothing else to say, she dipped her head and all but ran towards the door.

Chapter Fifteen

Georgiana, Viscountess Endersley, was a large woman, impressive both in size and in physical appearance. She had the most incredible red hair Helen had ever seen, a complexion that appeared almost white in comparison, and pale green eyes that watched the movements of all around her with the unblinking stare of a hawk. Her gown of dark maroon satin had surely been created by one of London's foremost modesties, and she carried herself with the air of a woman who was used to being in control—of herself *and* of everyone else around her.

'So, Gillian, you are to be wed at last,' the grand lady commented when everyone was gathered in the drawing-room before dinner. 'I am very pleased to hear it. And to young Riddleston, no less. Excellent. You have done very well for yourself, my dear. Very well.'

'Thank you, Aunt Georgiana,' Gillian answered dutifully.

'How old are you now, child?'

'Seventeen, aunt.'

Lady Endersley nodded. 'A good age for a gel to

be married. I m'self was married at seventeen. Doesn't do for a young woman to remain single too long. Would you not agree, Mrs Llewellyn?'

Sophie, who was standing in the company of her husband, Rhys, nodded her agreement. 'I certainly have no argument with that, Aunt Georgiana.'

'There, you see, Gillian. Your stepsister is happily wed and I daresay you shall be as well. Nigel Riddleston is a fine young man. One day, he will inherit the family fortunes and estates, and you shall become mistress of Kestwick Park. So, when is the wedding to take place?'

'In a fortnight's time,' Gillian told her, 'after which we plan to travel north to Scotland for a few weeks, and then spend Christmas in Wiltshire. We should be in London by March.'

'Splendid. You must call upon me there and I shall take you around. You will no doubt wish to refurbish a house, and my ability to acquaint you with which merchants to visit and which to avoid will go a long way towards saving you considerable time and money.'

'Thank you, Aunt Georgiana.'

Satisfied, Lady Endersley turned her attention towards Helen, who was standing quietly at Gillian's side. 'I do not believe I have made the acquaintance of this person, Gillian?'

'No, aunt, you have not. Pray allow me to introduce my very good friend, Miss Helen de Coverdale. Miss de Coverdale, my aunt, Lady Endersley.'

Helen gracefully curtsied. 'Lady Endersley.'

'*Miss* de Coverdale?' the Viscountess repeated in surprise. 'You are not married? But…surely you are of an age to be.'

'Yes, my lady, I suppose I am.'

'But how singular.' Lady Endersley glanced at Oliver, who had recently come over to join them. 'What is wrong with young men today, Oliver, that they would leave a beautiful young woman like this to sit on the shelf?'

Oliver turned to Helen and gave her a smile that made her go weak at the knees. 'I cannot imagine, Aunt. Except to say that perhaps Miss de Coverdale is not inclined towards marriage.'

'Not inclined towards marriage! Nonsense, all young women are inclined towards marriage. You have a most unusual surname, Miss de Coverdale,' the Viscountess remarked. 'Does your family reside in Hertfordshire?'

'No, ma'am. My parents are both gone and I live in…a small village in Northamptonshire.'

'Really. And have you other family there?'

'No, I live alone. That is—' Helen went to explain when she saw the look of concern on Gillian's face and abruptly stopped. Why was the child frowning? Was she worried about what Lady Endersley might say when she learned the truth of what she was?

'Miss de Coverdale is an exceptional watercolourist, Aunt Georgiana,' Oliver said in a conversational tone. 'She is also fluent in Italian, and is presently engaged in the teaching of those subjects at a private girls' school in Northamptonshire.'

'A girls' school!'

'Yes. The establishment has an excellent reputation and is run by a woman who is herself an acknowledged historian, poet and novelist.'

'Good Lord.' Lady Endersley's eyes widened in

astonishment. 'This young woman is a schoolmis-tress?'

'Yes. She is also Gillian's friend,' Oliver said in a voice that dared anyone to offer a criticism. 'Sophie and I were both very pleased that she accepted our invitation to come.'

There was a long, heavy silence. Lady Endersley glanced at Sophie, then at Helen, and then finally at Oliver, who was still standing relaxed and at ease in front of her.

'Well, I suppose it is not for me to comment upon who you invite to your house, Oliver, but in my day, we did *not* invite caper merchants and tutors to join in our family celebrations.' Lady Endersley looked down her nose at Helen, and then turned to address her next remark to her nephew. 'By the by, I saw Lady Merriot and her daughter in town last week. Constance has become quite the elegant young lady. So poised and refined. And of course, she always was beautiful. In fact, I seem to remember you saying that she was the most beautiful young lady you had ever seen. Is that not correct?'

Oliver's mouth curved in a knowing smile. 'I likely said as much, yes.'

'I thought so. I told her I would pass along her greetings. I also told her you would likely call upon her when you were next in London.'

The last remark was accompanied by a look at Helen that no one—including Helen—could fail to understand. Clearly, Lady Endersley was informing everyone that while Oliver might think well enough of Helen to invite her to celebrate his ward's be-trothal, she was *not* to be mistaken for a lady who might engage his affections in any other way.

And Helen knew there was nothing Oliver or anyone else could say that was going to change her mind
about that!

The rest of the evening did not improve. Though
the meal was excellent, the wines exceptional, and the
conversation filled with details about wedding break-
fasts and house plans, the atmosphere was still
strained. Mrs Llewellyn's seating arrangement thankfully put Helen at the opposite end of the table from
the Viscountess, but it did not lessen her discomfort
at being there. Because every time Helen looked up,
she saw people staring at her, their expressions rang-
ing from mildly pitying to outright condemning.

Was it any wonder she pleaded a headache and
retired as early as possible?

Gillian, of course, had valiantly tried to ease the
situation. She had caught up with Helen at the bottom
of the stairs and tried to assure her that she mustn't
pay any attention to Lady Endersley's remarks, reminding her—as Oliver had done—that one of the
Viscountess's own daughters-in-law was the offspring
of a lowly clergyman. But Helen had merely smiled
and assured Gillian that she was not offended by the
woman's remarks, and that she truly was suffering
from a headache. What would have been the point in
saying anything else?

Lady Endersley was Oliver's aunt; a member of the
aristocracy, and a woman of considerable influence
and power in society. How could Helen blame her for
harbouring cynical opinions about her, an impoverished schoolmistress? The Viscountess obviously
viewed her as an unmarried woman who was desirous
of bettering her circumstances in life, and who saw

in Oliver a way of making that happen. Perhaps she even believed that the only reason Helen was here was so that Oliver might be able to visit with her under the guise of her being a guest at Gillian's betrothal party. The fact that Oliver had intervened on her behalf would only have served to confirm the woman's suspicions. After all, why else would her beloved nephew—a man who could have had any lady he desired—defend the reputation of a penniless schoolmistress unless she already meant something to him?

No, it was better that she have as little to do with Lady Endersley as possible, Helen decided. She had no desire to be humiliated in front of Oliver or Mrs Llewellyn again, and if she kept to her room and did not venture downstairs, there would be no chance of that happening.

As to the ball tomorrow night, she would mingle as little as possible, make sure that she kept as far away from the Viscountess and her family as possible, and first thing Saturday morning, she would climb back into the carriage and head for home, where her associations with Oliver Brandon would become nothing more than a collection of bittersweet memories.

Helen found the gown she intended to wear to the betrothal party tucked away at the back of the wardrobe and wrapped in layers of tissue thin paper. Curiosity compelled her to draw it out, but from the moment she removed its wrappings and held it up to the light, Helen knew it was perfect.

The rich, ivory-coloured silk was exquisite, its fine overlay of silver net shimmering in the morning sun.

Hundreds of tiny beads had been sewn into the bodice and down the front in a narrow line, and though the styling of the gown was years out of date, its uncomplicated design made it relatively simple to alter. All that was required was some gathering of the fabric around the bust line, the application of some lace around the sleeves and neck, and the shortening of the hem to make it appear *au courant*.

Mrs Llewellyn, after deciding not to press Helen into coming downstairs, personally brought her something to eat, and after seeing what she was working on, kindly sent up a pair of long ivory gloves for Helen to wear. Gillian also appeared at her door late in the afternoon with the gift of a beautiful, hand-painted fan, something Helen knew would go perfectly with the gown and which Gillian assured her she was delighted to see her wearing.

'And I shall send Marie to assist you this evening,' the girl said as she flounced down upon the bed. 'I am positively dying to see what she will do with all that wonderful long hair of yours.'

Helen smiled, but the expression in her eyes was wistful. 'I haven't had anyone dress my hair in years. Since I was your age, in fact.'

'Really?' Gillian's eyes went wide. 'Then you haven't always been a teacher?'

Helen set the fan on the bedside table and shook her head. 'At one time, my life was not unlike yours. I went to parties and to musicales. I even sang and played the piano forte.'

'You never told me!'

'I had no reason to. My life is not what it once was.'

'But you were obviously comfortable with this sort

of thing once, so there is no reason for you to feel uncomfortable tonight. And I do so want you to have a good time, Miss de Coverdale, the presence of my aunt notwithstanding.'

'I shall have a wonderful time, whether your aunt is there or not,' Helen said as bravely as she could. 'Because more than anything, I am looking forward to seeing *you* dance with the young man whom Mrs Llewellyn tells me you are very happy to be marrying.'

Gillian sighed. 'Yes, I am really most fortunate. Mr Riddleston treats me ever so well, and he is very handsome. Did Sophie tell you we met in London last year?'

'Yes. She also told me you were not taken with the gentleman upon first acquaintance.'

Gillian tipped back her head and laughed. 'Yes, is that not a good joke? I cannot even recall what he was like the first time I met him. But strangely enough, when I saw him again last month, it was almost as though…I was seeing him for the first time. As though he was a different person altogether.'

Neglecting to point out that it was probably Gillian who was the different person, Helen said only, 'Do you love him?'

Gillian's smile slipped ever so slightly. 'Yes. Perhaps not in the way I loved Mr Wymington, but I would never tell Oliver that. He has been so good to me since we've been back, Miss de Coverdale. He's taken me out nearly every day, and he has spoiled me even more than he did before. In fact, I shall almost be sorry to leave Shefferton Hall,' she admitted with a laugh. 'As to Mr Wymington…well…I know that he was only interested in my fortune, and I know that should make it easier for me to get over him, but a person never *really* forgets their first love, do they?'

Unbidden, an image of Thomas's face flashed into Helen's mind, and for the first time in her life, she realised she couldn't see him any more. His features were beginning to blur, and the memory of his voice and of his physical appearance was becoming hazy in her mind. But she saw Oliver's face. She saw it as clearly as though he was standing right in front of her.

'We can if we allow ourselves to,' Helen said softly. 'In time, your memories of Mr Wymington will fade as new ones of your life with your husband and children move in to take their place. But no one can say how long that will take. Only you will know when it happens. But now, we must put the past aside and look to the future. I am here to celebrate your engagement to Mr Riddleston. And now before you dash away to get dressed and become the most popular young lady in the house tonight, I insist that you tell me everything you can about him!'

At twenty minutes to eight, Helen closed the door to her room and quietly tiptoed downstairs. She had no desire to be on the upper floors when the guests began to arrive. Better to be down here, tucked away in some quiet corner where no one would see her, and where she could lose herself in the crowds of people that would quickly gather.

Would she feel terribly ill at ease this evening, Helen wondered as she made her way into the deserted parlour? In truth, she failed to see how she could not. It had been years since she had moved in any kind of society, and though she had long ago learned the necessary social skills, she could only pray that she would remember how to use them.

Thank goodness she need have no concerns about her appearance. The gown had turned out even better than she'd hoped. The shimmering fabric now draped softly over the fullness of her breasts, fit snugly underneath and then fell in graceful folds to the floor. The elegant evening gloves Mrs Llewellyn had lent her for the occasion were perfect, and Gillian's beautiful hand-painted fan hung from a ribbon at her wrist.

True to her word, Gillian had also sent her maid to attend to Helen's hair, and the pretty French girl had worked wonders with it. She had exclaimed at length over its lush softness, and after studying it for a few moments, had decided to dress it in the antique Roman style, bringing the gleaming tresses together and confining them at the back of Helen's head. A single ribbon of ivory silk studded with pearl ornaments wound like a ribbon of starlight through the dark tresses.

Helen could scarce believe that she was the same woman who had left Steep Abbot only a day before. Certainly she did not look the same. In her beautiful gown and her upswept hairstyle, she looked as though she belonged in this magnificent house, with its beautiful, sophisticated people.

And just for tonight, Helen *wanted* to believe that she belonged. Because more than anything, she wanted Oliver to see her as something other than a schoolmistress wearing a plain old schoolmistress's gown. Just for tonight, she wanted him to see her as the privileged young lady she had once been.

'I vow the girls and the staff at Mrs Guarding's Academy would not recognise you, Miss de

Coverdale,' Oliver said softly from the door. 'I almost did not myself.'

The soft, caressing tone caused Helen to gasp as she spun around. She hadn't heard him come into the room, but now as she saw him standing opposite her, she could only thank the Fates for having given her this last opportunity to spend time with the man who had become so important in her life.

He had dressed formally for the occasion and Helen knew that he would be the most handsome man in the house. His double-breasted black cut-away coat, tailored, no doubt, by Weston or Meyer, fit his broad shoulders to perfection, while light kerseymere breeches and fine silk stockings outlined as fine a leg as Helen had ever seen. A snowy white cravat nestled against the lapels of his jacket, the arrangement of which she knew would have taken considerable time and skill, whilst nestled in the folds was an elegant sapphire pin.

Oliver's appearance was impeccable, and yet now, as in the past, there was nothing of the dandy about him. He appeared to her at this moment exactly as he always had; a simple man of taste and refinement. It was no wonder Lady Endersley held out such high hopes for him.

'You startled me, Mr Brandon,' Helen said, hating the breathlessness that had crept back into her voice.

Oliver bowed from the waist. 'Forgive me, Miss de Coverdale, it was not my intention to do so. I should have noticed that you were lost in your thoughts.' He smiled as he moved towards her. 'But I am surprised to find you hidden away in here. I thought to see you coming down the stairs. You would have created quite a stir looking as beautiful as you do now.'

Helen felt a blush heat her skin, and hastily opened her fan. 'I thought only to find an out-of-the-way place to hide. I am well aware my company is not so grand as many of the guests who will be here tonight.'

If possible, Oliver's smile grew gentler still. 'Ah, but your presence is more welcome than most, Miss de Coverdale, because *you* were invited out of affection. Would that I could say that about everyone who will be coming tonight.'

Helen's mouth curved in a grateful smile. 'Then I shall consider myself fortunate, sir, for I would far rather be thought of with affection than obligation.'

Oliver chuckled, and Helen was relieved to discover that she could still converse in the light, flirtatious manner expected of young men and women. The only problem was, she had no desire to flirt with Oliver. Her feelings went too deep for such trivial exchanges. As she moved around the room, she was extremely conscious of being alone with him. It seemed to her that his presence filled every inch of the room, and yet it was in no way suffocating or overwhelming.

But then, how could it be? He was the man she had fallen in love with. The man she would have chosen to spend the rest of her life with. As long as she could be in his company, there was no other place in the world she would rather be.

'You must be...very pleased that Gillian accepted Mr Riddleston's proposal so quickly,' Helen said, hoping to engage him in harmless conversation.

'Pleased *and* relieved,' Oliver admitted. 'I am delighted that Gillian is promised to a gentleman whom I can admire and who I know is marrying her for the right reasons. But at the same time, I am relieved that she genuinely cares for him and is happy to go through with the marriage for her own sake.'

'Go *through* with it?' Helen's expression reflected her surprise. 'You make it sound as though she was doing something she would rather not.'

Oliver sighed. 'Come, Miss de Coverdale, you and I know each other—and the situation—too well for that. Gillian is happy enough to be marrying young Riddleston, and I know she holds him in great affection, but I do not believe she feels for him the kind of breathless passion she felt for Sidney Wymington. Wymington was the kind of man whose appearance and manner would inspire such a response in the female breast. Even you cannot deny that he was a dashing fellow.'

'No, I cannot,' Helen admitted with a smile. 'But the flaws I discovered in his character soon blinded me to his good looks. My unfortunate conversation with him in Abbot Giles, and his attempts to discredit me in front of you and Miss Gresham, made me see him as a most unattractive man all around.'

'I would be lying if I said I was not glad to hear you say so,' Oliver said quietly. 'Fortunately, Nigel Riddleston has nothing of Wymington's ways about him, yet he is every bit as charming and a hundred times more sincere. In time he will inherit a grand estate and I know he has the intelligence and foresight to manage it well. He will not be one to fritter away his fortune on impulse and trifles.'

'And is he as…enamoured of Gillian as she is of him?' Helen asked, careful to use the same word he had.

'The poor lad is head over heels in love with her. Has been ever since the first time he saw her in

London.' Oliver's mouth curved in a smile. 'Yes, I am well pleased with the way events have turned out for Gillian, especially when I remember how perilously close we came to losing her. But what about you, Miss de Coverdale? Have matters turned out as well for you as you might have liked?'

Helen drew a long, deep breath. The question begged a cautious answer, for while she had no wish to lie to him outright, she could hardly admit the truth of her feelings.

'I am in the enviable position of having both a home and a job at the Guarding Academy,' she said slowly, 'and I am fortunate enough to have earned the respect and affection of a few good friends. What more could a woman in my position want?'

'The same things any woman might want,' Oliver replied. 'A home of your own. Children to care for. A husband to love—'

'Oliver, is that you I hear?' Mrs Llewellyn's voice called, seconds before she breezed into the room. 'The receiving line is forming and Gillian wishes you to take your place. You should—why, Miss de Coverdale, whatever are you doing here? And looking so very beautiful.' Sophie's eyes widened as she took in the magnificence of the skilfully altered gown. 'I vow, you have worked a minor miracle, my dear. Does she not look radiant, Oliver?'

'She does indeed.' Oliver's gaze fell softly on Helen's face. 'I told her as much only a moment ago.'

'But why are you not out in the ballroom where the gentlemen can see you?'

Helen felt the blush begin at her throat and spread upwards. 'I did not wish to appear too early amongst your guests, Mrs Llewellyn. Lady Endersley—'

'Oh, bother Lady Endersley,' Mrs Llewellyn interrupted. 'I intend to keep her fully occupied and well away from you this evening, my dear. But there will be many others anxious to make your acquaintance. And the sooner you take your place amongst them, the sooner you shall begin enjoying yourself. Now, Oliver, off you go. I shall attend to Miss de Coverdale.' Sophie marched forward and linked her arm through Helen's. 'It is past time we introduced this lovely young woman to society. And of course, to our delightful Mr Riddleston.'

Chapter Sixteen

Nigel Riddleston was everything Helen hoped he would be. He was handsome, well-spoken, and so in love with Gillian that it nearly brought tears to Helen's eyes.

Oh yes, he would make her a wonderful husband. There was a quiet sincerity about him that was eminently appealing, and as the evening progressed, Helen was better able to understand why Oliver was so impressed with him. While Gillian tended to flit around the crowded room like a beautiful butterfly, Mr Riddleston took his time walking amongst the guests, stopping to speak to as many of them as he could and always with a kind word and a genuine smile. While Gillian was frequently sought out by other single gentlemen for dances, Mr Riddleston seemed perfectly content to watch from the side. But he always knew where she was. He was there, watchful, but never hovering, and Helen knew it was pride rather than possession that kept him glancing in her direction.

'Is he not a sweet man, Miss de Coverdale?' Gillian asked when the two of them at last had an opportunity to be alone. 'I admit, I did not expect to like him near so well as I do, but I find the more I come to know him, the more there is to admire about him.'

'He is a very likeable young man indeed,' Helen said, delighted at the note of happiness in Gillian's voice. 'I am more pleased for you than I can say. And you are to be married in a fortnight. How excited you must be.'

'Yes. I had originally thought the spring would be nice, but Nigel would like to be married by Christmas so that we can take up residence in London early in the new year. His mother and father keep a house in town and they have given it to us as a wedding present. Is that not exceedingly generous of them?'

'It is generous indeed.'

'And I expect *you* to come and visit us very often. You will come, won't you, Miss de Coverdale?' Gillian's eyes were softly beseeching. 'I should like that above all.'

'I shall do my very best,' Helen assured her. 'But you must remember that it is not always easy for a schoolmistress to leave her classes.'

'Then I must do everything I can to ensure that you do not remain a schoolmistress much longer! When you come to London, I shall introduce you to every handsome, eligible gentleman I know.'

Amused by the girl's emphatic if somewhat naïve declaration, Helen began to laugh. 'Oh, Gillian, that is a very kind sentiment, but I doubt any of the handsome, eligible gentlemen you are likely to know will have any interest in making the acquaintance of a one-and-thirty-year-old schoolmistress from Steep Abbot.'

Gillian looked appalled. 'But how can you say

that? Only look at the way the gentlemen are watching you tonight. Have you not noticed the way their eyes follow you around? Several perfectly amiable young men have asked me about you, and Sir Peter Rollings wishes to be introduced. He told me he thought you were quite the most beautiful woman he had ever seen.'

'What's this I hear, Gillie?' Oliver interrupted. 'Are you trying to lure Miss de Coverdale away? Mrs Guarding will not thank you for depriving her of yet another teacher.'

Gillian rolled her eyes. 'Really, Oliver. I would far rather see Miss de Coverdale married to a man who loves her than be locked away at some girls' school where she is forced to teach watercolours and Italian to a bunch of simpering young misses for the rest of her life. She is far too beautiful for that, don't you think?'

Helen blushed furiously. 'I am sure Mr Brandon has no opinion on the matter, Miss Gresham. But look there, I believe Mr Riddleston is attempting to secure your attention.'

Gillian turned and waved at the young man, who was indeed smiling and signalling in her direction. 'Yes, he wishes me to talk to his sister, the young lady standing there on his right. Amanda is a rather plain creature, but she has a sweet temper and I love her dearly. No doubt he will wish me to see to her Season once we are wed. But do not forget what I said, Miss de Coverdale.' Impulsively, Gillian reached up and kissed Helen on the cheek. 'I shall do everything I can to see that *you* are soon married as well. And thank you for being such a wonderful friend. I am so very glad you are here.' Then, in a rustle of silk skirts, she hurried away, leaving Helen, flushed and embarrassed, standing alone in the company of Oliver Brandon again.

'You must forgive Gillian for being a trifle outspoken,' Oliver said into the somewhat awkward silence. 'She tends to speak her mind about whatever happens to be on it at the time.'

'Yes. I suppose we must put it down to...the excitement of the evening,' Helen said, desperately trying to make light of the episode. 'She hardly knows what she is saying.'

'She is right about one thing, though. You are far too beautiful to remain a teacher for the rest of your life.'

Helen's pulse skittered as she opened her fan and plied it fervently to her cheeks. 'You are...too kind, sir.'

'I told you once before that kindness has very little to do with what I say to you, Miss de Coverdale.' Oliver clasped his hands behind his back in the gesture Helen had come to know so well. 'I am simply speaking the truth. You are a beautiful woman and there isn't a man in this room who doesn't know it.'

Helen swallowed hard. She knew she should offer some witty, sophisticated remark, but in the face of Oliver's compliment, she could think of nothing. What a pity. It seemed her newly reclaimed social skills had already deserted her.

'Gillian told me that...it was Mr Riddleston's wish that they marry before Christmas,' she said instead, saying the first thing that came to mind.

'Yes, he is anxious to get on with it. But then, as I told you, he has been in love with her for some time. Indeed, I think it was a case of love at first sight.'

Helen watched the young pair across the floor, and inadvertently, a soft sigh escaped her lips. 'I do hope it lasts, for both their sakes.'

'Oh, I think it will. It has happened in our family a number of times.'

'Yes, I remember you telling me that your sister and her husband fell in love that way.'

'Yes. As did I.'

A bolt of lightning striking the floor beside her could not have startled Helen more. The quietly offered words, spoken in a conversational tone of voice, caused her pulse to quicken and her breath to come in short gasps. 'I…beg your pardon?'

'You sound surprised, Miss de Coverdale. Did you not think I was the type who could fall in love at first sight?'

'I'm sure I have…no idea what type you are, Mr Brandon.' *Oliver was in love?* Oh, dear God, how could such a thing be true! Why hadn't Gillian told her? Surely the girl had known that her own stepbrother was harbouring a *tendre* for someone. Especially one that had been going on for some time. Why had she led her to believe there had been no one in his life?

'I must confess to being…surprised, Mr Brandon,' Helen stammered, fighting to keep her voice steady. 'Gillian did not…tell me you were involved with anyone.'

'She did not tell you because she did not know,' Oliver said with a smile. 'No one does. It happened a long time ago.'

'I see. And what of the…young lady?' she asked,

forcing herself to say the words. 'How does she feel about your keeping silent for such a long time?'

'I have no idea,' Oliver replied. 'Because the young lady doesn't know how I feel either.'

Helen could barely hear him over the strange buzzing in her head. 'But how can that be, sir? If you were…in love with her, she must have had *some* indication as to your feelings?'

'In truth, she had none. Because at the time, she didn't know me from Adam.'

The buzzing was replaced by a dull roar. 'Surely there was something in the way you spoke to her—'

'I said not a word to the lady,' Oliver admitted quietly. 'It would not have been…appropriate at the time. Nor was I given an opportunity to do so. But the memory of her face and the manner of our first meeting has stayed with me to this very day.'

Helen wished she could think of something to say, but her mind had gone totally blank. What was she supposed to say upon learning that the man she had fallen in love with was in love with someone else?

'I know it sounds strange, Miss de Coverdale, but you have to understand that my feelings were of the kind I thought best kept to myself,' Oliver continued as the silence between them lengthened. 'As I said, I was not even willing to acknowledge my own awareness of them at the time. And because so many years went by before I saw the lady again, I had no reason to believe they still existed. But then, under the most amazing of circumstances, I saw her again and I realised that, to my great astonishment, nothing had changed. I felt the same way about her as I had upon seeing her that very first time.' Oliver shook his head in wonderment. 'It was unsettling to say the least.'

Unsettling indeed, Helen echoed silently, aware that any pleasure she might have taken in the night was now completely gone. All she felt was sick at heart; numbed by the painful realisation that Oliver would never be anything to her but the most casual of acquaintances. Saddened, because she had foolishly allowed herself to believe since coming to Shefferton Hall that he held her in some esteem. Now, knowing that he did not, she wanted nothing more than to run away and hide before she made a complete fool of herself.

'Mr Brandon, would you please…excuse me? I find it very warm in the room all of a sudden.'

'Of course, Miss de Coverdale, but is everything all right? You seem a little distressed. Perhaps you would care to take a stroll on the terrace?'

'Yes. That would be…most welcome,' Helen said, grasping at anything that would serve as a means of escaping his company.

'Then allow me to escort you outside.'

She blanched. 'No! That is…thank you, sir, but the offer of an escort is not necessary. I can manage…quite well on my own.'

'I think not, dear lady,' Oliver said softly. 'Your face has suddenly turned the colour of your gown and I fear you are in danger of fainting away if you keep breathing like that. Come, allow me to escort you on to the terrace. A change of scenery and a breath of fresh air might be just the thing to revive you.'

Helen wanted to tell him it was going to take a great deal more than fresh air and scenery to revive her, but what would be the point? Nothing was going to change the fact that Oliver Brandon was in love with someone else.

Thankfully, the evening air did help restore her equilibrium, if not her spirits. Helen closed her eyes and drew a few deep breaths of the cool night air into her lungs and felt the light-headedness begin to ease. But it did nothing to lessen the feelings of despair within her heart. That only grew stronger every time she looked at Oliver's dear face and knew that he was lost to her.

She gripped the stone balustrade hard, desperately trying to hide the trembling in her hands, knowing that the sooner she could get away from him, the better.

'There, do you not feel a little better for having come outside?' Oliver asked, his voice low and filled with concern.

Helen dropped her head to hide the expression in her eyes, and wished she might be anywhere but here. She did not even have the strength to *look* at him. 'Thank you, Mr Brandon, you are very kind to be so attentive. And yes, I…believe I am feeling…a little better. Forgive me. I am not used to crowds and it has been…a very long time since I attended a function like this. I think the excitement of the evening quite overwhelmed me.'

'Of course. Your reaction was only to be expected. But are you warm enough? There is a chill in the air tonight.'

'Thank you, I am fine. But it would probably be best if you were to…return to your guests, Mr Brandon. People will be wondering where you are.'

'Let them wonder. It is Gillian's celebration, not mine,' he reminded her. 'And right now, I don't care about anyone else, Miss de Coverdale.' He put his hands on her shoulders and gently turned her to face him. 'I only care about you.'

Helen gasped, dismayed to feel tears trembling on her lashes. 'But you *don't* care. You are in love with…someone else. You just told me as much!'

His burning eyes held her still. 'Does that disturb you?'

'Yes. *No!* I mean…of course it doesn't disturb me.' She dashed her hand across her eyes, wiping the traitorous moisture away. 'Why should it?'

'Because my dear Miss de Coverdale, I am hoping that you are *not* as indifferent to me as you have been trying to make me believe.' His fingers tightened on her arms. 'Please tell me you aren't, *amore*.'

Stunned, Helen gazed up into his face. 'I *beg* your pardon?'

Slowly and seductively, Oliver's eyes slid over her face, lingering on her eyes before coming to rest briefly on her lips. 'Do you not know the word?'

'Of course I know the word. But…why would you call me your beloved when you have just finished telling me that you are…that you are…'

'In love with someone else? Why indeed? Unless it is because I thought it was time the young lady was made aware of it herself.'

Helen stared up at him, wondering if she had somehow fallen asleep and was dreaming all this. 'Mr Brandon, pray do not tease me. In my present state, I am ill-equipped to deal with the subtleties of your phrasing. Please, tell me what you mean—'

'I mean, sweet Helen, that *you* are the woman I'm in love with. The same woman I've been in love with for so many long, empty years. Do you find that so very hard to believe?'

At that moment, Helen was extremely grateful for the strength of his hands on her arms. Otherwise, she feared she might have sunk to the ground in a heap. Oliver Brandon was in *love* with her? With *her*?

'But…you thought I was…immoral,' she whispered as the tears began to roll down her cheeks. 'You accused me of having…a bad influence on Gillian.'

'Yes, because I had convinced myself you would. But in my heart, I knew differently.' He reached into his pocket and drew out his handkerchief. 'I never forgot the first time I saw you, Helen. That night, in the library, when you looked up and saw me, I knew then that something had happened to me. That the memory of your face would stay with me for the rest of my life. But I never put it down to my being in love with you.'

Helen sniffed. 'You didn't?'

'Of course not. I thought I had been bewitched by a pair of beautiful dark eyes.' He smiled as he gently wiped away the traces of her tears. 'I convinced myself you couldn't possibly be the kind of woman I wanted to marry because it seemed to me that we were different in so many ways. And yet, when I saw you again that morning at Mrs Guarding's Academy, I knew it to be a lie.'

'But when you spoke to me in the carriage,' Helen persisted, 'when you came to take me driving, you told me that I…that I—'

'I know what I said,' Oliver cut in. 'And I wish to God I could take back every single word I uttered. I never meant to hurt you, beloved. I think that in some way, I was still fighting what I was feeling for you. I couldn't deny that Fate had brought us back together again, but I was tempted to think of it as a cruel joke rather than the best thing that could have happened to me.' He reached for her hand and held it in his. 'Tell me I'm not harbouring foolish hopes, dearest. Tell me that you care for me, even if only a little. For even that will give me a reason to keep on trying to make you love me.'

'Oh, Oliver, you have no need of such foolish hopes,' Helen told him weakly. 'I love you more than you know. More than I can possibly tell you. But I never imagined you were in love with me. I never thought—'

It was as far as Helen got. Oliver silenced her words with a kiss of such soul-searing passion that it left her breathless and trembling with emotion. Everything and everyone else faded away as his lips closed over hers and his arms drew her close, bringing their bodies into intimate contact and arousing feelings and sensations that Helen had never experienced before. It was as though they were the only two people in the world. The only two people who mattered.

'I never want to hear that mentioned between us again,' Oliver said when at last he raised his head and gazed down into her eyes. 'I never want to hear you talk about Lord Talbot or your poor clergyman, or any other man who has ever spoken to you in a disrespectful way, lest I be tempted to seek out every one of them and challenge them all to a duel!'

'Dear me, challenge them *all*?' Helen's laughter escaped as a soft ripple of sound. 'If that is the case, I fear you will be too busy fighting to spend any time with me.'

'Ah, but if you will have me, dearest Helen, I intend to spend the rest of my life as close to you as I am now. And I guarantee, there will be times when you may wish me far away, so devoted will my attentions be.'

'Never! I could never wish you far away from me again. In fact, if I had only one wish, it would be that you would not be more than ten paces from my side. I love you, Oliver. A separation of even a short time would be cruel punishment indeed.'

'Then...will you marry me, Helen?' he whispered, as his fingers touched her face and moved tenderly along her cheek. 'Will you consent to be my wife?'

Helen closed her eyes and leaned into his caress. 'I would marry you in an instant, beloved, but...I must ask if you have given this question the consideration it deserves.'

'What is there to consider, other than how we feel about each other?'

Helen sighed. 'There is much to consider, given that our positions in life are so different. You must know there are others who will not be as well pleased with your decision as I.'

'Others?' His brow darkened. 'What others?'

'Lady Endersley for one.'

'Lady Endersley be damned!'

'No, you must not say that, Oliver,' Helen said, gently pressing her fingers to his lips. 'She is not wrong to care about you, nor is she wrong to wish to see you marry well. She is your aunt, and she loves you. But by marrying me, you may risk losing her affection, and I would hate to be the cause of such a rift between you.'

Oliver stared at her for a long time. So long, in fact, that Helen began to wonder if he was indeed reflecting upon the wisdom of his choice. But when he spoke again, she knew that nothing had changed.

'Dearest Helen. With everything you say, you only make me love you more. You are not wrong in wishing to make me look beyond my own feelings. And you are not wrong in saying that others may not be pleased with my decision. But it is *my* decision to make, and our happiness that is at stake. I've found the woman I want to marry. She teaches watercolours and Italian at a girls' school in Steep Abbot. And if my aunt or any other members of my family will not receive her, then they shall not be received by me.' Oliver drew her close and with infinite tenderness cupped her chin between his fingers and tipped it back. 'I love this lady so very much. And if she will agree to have me, I intend to spend the rest of my life showing her exactly how much I do love her, in every way I can. Do you think, under the circumstances, that will be convincing enough?'

Helen's eyes glowed with a deep and abiding sense of happiness. 'Oh yes, my darling Oliver. I think that, under any circumstances, that is probably all the convincing the lady is ever likely to need.'

Modern Romance™
...seduction and
passion guaranteed

Tender Romance™
...love affairs that
last a lifetime

Sensual Romance™
...sassy, sexy and
seductive

Blaze
...sultry days and
steamy nights

Medical Romance™
...medical drama on
the pulse

Historical Romance™
...rich, vivid and
passionate

29 new titles every month.

*With all kinds of Romance for
every kind of mood...*

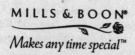

MILLS & BOON®

Makes any time special™

MAT4

Treat yourself this Mother's Day to the ultimate indulgence

3 brand new romance novels and a box of chocolates

= only £7.99

Available from 15th February

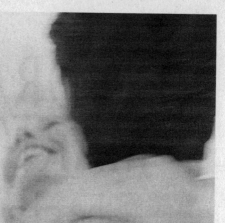

Starting Over

Another chance at love...
Found where least expected

PENNY
JORDAN

Published 15th February

*Available at most branches of WH Smith,
Tesco, Martins, Borders, Eason, Sainsbury's
and most good paperback bookshops.*